Hot Rucking Canadian

GABBI GREY

T ravis

After a hard day's work at my construction job, I decide to head to a gay bar to hook up. Then the man of my dreams walks in—tall, dark, handsome, and totally built. Sounds like a fairy tale. And maybe it is. We have one unforgettable night, then I steal away in the night, because I don't do repeats. But when I see him on television the next day, I realize I haven't had my fill of the sexy rugby player. He might not want to see me again, after I ditched him, but I have to try.

Isaiah

Waking up alone after a night of spectacular sex isn't the end of the world. I shouldn't feel lonely. After all, I've got my squad—my best friends on and off the pitch. I've also got my mom, whom I love, and my dad's family back in New Zealand. I'm playing pro rugby for adoring fans in Vancouver, my dream come true. Having one hookup leave me without so much as thanks and goodbye shouldn't hurt. But when he reappears at a game, I'm in big trouble. No one ever made me want them like this, after just one night. If I let Travis into my life again, am I just courting heartbreak the next time he walks away?

Hot Rucking Canadian is a 26k novella about a rugby fullback who embraces life, a grumpy construction worker who always sees the worst in life, and the love story that spans across an ocean.

multimedia, audio, or other medium. We support the right of humans to control their artistic works.

No generative AI was used in the creation of this book.

Edits by ELF

Cover design by The Cover Fling

Dedication

Jenny & Andie

Sofia & Anna

ELF

Wendy

Renae

Contents

Chapter One

Travis

"You riding home tonight, Travis?" Jemima eyed me with those otherworldly blue eyes of hers.

"Yep." I tapped my helmet on the chair next to me.

"One, and then water." She snagged a glass, poured me a sleeve of beer, and placed it before me.

Some nights I grabbed transit here, drank like a fish, and slid into a cab for the ride home. Expensive nights, those, but well worth it. Those were nights I assumed I'd be going home alone.

Tonight, against all odds, I hoped for something different. "Thanks Jemi."

"You bet."

Her weird accent was something I hadn't ever been able to place, and I'd never bothered asking. I was also pretty certain she was queer, but I'd never asked about that either.

She just sort of manned the bar and left me in peace. Occasionally, though, she'd point out someone she thought I might hook up with.

Hook up.

Because that's all guys ever wanted to do with me. No one looked at the tats, earrings, facial scar, and perpetual scowl, and thought, *yeah, there's the guy I want to spend the rest of my life with.*

That was fair.

Jemima once—just once—suggested maybe if I smiled more, I might get lucky. I was allowed to smile in her gay bar, she maintained.

The bar that was on the seedier side of both town and less chic than some of the other upscale places on Davie Street in downtown Vancouver.

I worked in the core of the city, doing construction each day. Escaping to the east end felt like traveling a million miles. I preferred not to go back, even for the promise of getting laid.

Not to say I didn't venture over some weekends. To see how the other half lived. I wouldn't have gone so far as to say I was an oddity—this was the gayest part of pretty much all of British Columbia—but I stood out. Sometimes in a good way and sometimes not.

"You looking tonight?" Jemima's blond hair swayed as she returned from delivering a drink to the other end of the bar.

As far as I could tell, she pretty much lived here. I'd never been in the place without finding her tending. "Do you ever get a break?" I squinted in the dim light.

She cackled. "Honey, you don't want to know what happens to this place when I'm not around."

Which didn't precisely answer my question. "Yeah, I'm looking."

"Maybe that cute ginger will come back. He was a looker." She fanned herself.

I winced. Yeah, Finn *had* been a looker.

Adorable redhead who had come in all the way from Cedar Valley, looking for a night of fun. He usually made his way over to Davie, but had decided to try this place for one night.

My lucky night.

Except he'd only been looking for a good time. He lived in Mission City—Vancouver was a bit of excitement in his life.

Personally, I thought being a firefighter was cool, but Finn had downplayed the day job.

He'd thought the rebar was exciting.

I'd refrained from talking about my day job. Doing ties all day required brute strength with very little in the brains department. I did what I was told to do. Once or twice, I questioned when something didn't seem right. And those times I'd been spot-on. But that was a couple of times in nearly two decades of work—so not all that impressive.

"Now there's a man I'd like to get to know better." Jemima gestured to the door with her chin.

Knowing Jemima's keen eye, slowly, deliberately, I pivoted my gaze. I wasn't so desperate as to gawk. I also wasn't too proud to show interest. At forty, I was way too old for games. A guy either wanted me or he didn't. I'd readily admit I wasn't picky. A lay was a lay. That attitude had landed me in hot water a couple of times, but I'd always managed.

Holy Mother of God.

Tall, broad, and built. A few inches above my own five-eight. Easily forty pounds more than me—mostly muscle. His shoulders were so wide, he nearly filled the doorway.

I was so scrawny that just about anyone could get past me easily.

Tanned skin. And, in the crappy lighting of the bar, I figured dark-brown eyes. That would fit. I couldn't figure heritage, but Vancouver had a bit of just about everything, and God knew, none of that mattered to me.

I licked my lips.

Jemima snickered.

Tall, broad, and built stepped into the room. After he caught my gaze, he ducked his head.

Oh God, he's shy. How adorable. At that moment, he also struck me as...submissive. No reason to know for certain, but his demeanor called to my inner Dominant. Most guys saw my tough exterior and, despite my size, pegged me as a Dom.

They weren't wrong.

If I'd been judging by stereotype, I would've pegged this guy as a Dominant as well.

And likely would be wrong.

He managed to meet my gaze again.

Slowly, I gestured to the empty seat next to me. My jeans grew tight.

Just as slowly, he approached. Looking a little like a deer caught in the headlights. Obviously he'd never been here before and, just as clearly, he was in way over his head.

"He's attracting some attention." Jemima placed a glass of water before me as she whispered the words. Then, like magic, she disappeared.

The guy eased up as he approached.

He's a marshmallow. Just an oversized teddy bear.

As he arrived at the barstool, though, he didn't sit.

Might as well make my move. "I'll follow you home. Go. Now."

A grin broke out on his face. "Yes, Sir."

And we're off.

Chapter Two

Isaiah

As I drove back to my condo in the west end, with a motorcycle rider hard on my ass, I kind of marveled at my luck.

First time I'd tried that bar.

My buddy on the team had mentioned it the other day.

Johnnie was always trying to set me up. He and Roger had a competition going as to who would be successful at helping me find my *forever man*.

I'd worried. Coming out as gay while playing on a professional rugby team.

In the end, though, I needn't have been concerned.

A couple of guys were...unimpressed.

Johnnie and Roger quickly put them in their place. Probably helped Johnnie was captain of the team and Roger had been with the team the longest.

Wonderful, they were dedicated to setting me up with guys.

Only...they always picked the wrong kind of men.

Awkward.

The guy in the bar tonight? Oh, sweet Lord, all the right kind of guy.

Size didn't matter to me. Looks absolutely never swayed me. No, I was looking for compatibility—as in me, wanting someone to tell me what to do. And, praying a little here, that he preferred to top.

I signaled and then turned into my parking garage.

He followed me into the underground.

I pointed to a visitor spot.

He gave a little nod and parked.

After I slid my own vehicle into a spot, I hustled to get out and make my way back to him.

He stood next to his sweet ride, with his helmet in his hands. His long, graying-brown hair was pulled back into a ponytail. His blue eyes sparkled mischief. His mouth turned up into a smile. Even his scar appeared less pronounced in the light of the garage. "You ready?"

"Yes, Sir."

"Great. You want to talk or just...?"

Of course I wanted to talk. I *always* wanted to talk. But talking might derail this—whatever *this* was—and in no way was I going to risk that. "I'm good with action."

He arched an eyebrow.

"Yes. That."

"I'm going to have you screaming." He pitched his voice low.

The garage was usually empty, but heat still crept into my cheeks as his words bounced off the concrete.

Then he moved closer. "I love that I can make you blush."

I tried really hard not to sniff. He had a soap-and-water vibe to him. No cologne or false scent.

Much like me. "I'm on the ninth floor."

"I like heights. There's nothing quite like seeing the city from the top of the world."

Unsure of what he meant, but also unwilling to wait much longer, I gestured to the entrance to the elevator lobby. We were two floors below ground, and so it would be eleven floors up. Eleven torturous floors.

"Yeah, let's do this." Another wicked grin.

He followed me, and I used my fob to get us to the elevators.

As always, neither elevator car was there, so we waited.

"I, uh, don't know your name." *Right, like that's not the dorkiest statement ever. Of course you don't know his name...he hasn't given it to you.*

Yet he grinned. "Badarse."

I blinked. "Excuse me?"

"You heard me."

"Yeah, but I've heard of badass before, but not—"

The bell chimed and the elevator door swept open.

We stepped inside.

I pressed the button for my floor, and the elevator began its climb upward. I lived in one of the older buildings on the westside—pretty much all I could afford.

"One of the guys on my crew, back when I was first starting, called me Badarse. He was Aussie."

"Crew?"

His nose twitched. "Construction."

Said with just enough edge to make it clear we weren't going to pursue this particular avenue of conversation.

I could take a hint. I didn't offer my name. Apparently we weren't going the intimacy route tonight. *Fine by me.*

Or so I told myself.

The bell chimed, and we exited the elevator. I gestured for him to follow me to 913. To my relief, he did. I hadn't been certain if I'd screwed things up by asking his name. Generally, in the throes of passion, I liked to use a guy's name. Upon reflection of this evening so far, I suspected *Sir* might go over quite well.

I unlocked the door and stepped in first so I could flip on the lights.

Then I stood aside to let him in.

I locked the door and before I could do anything, he was already removing his black leather biker boots. In response, I toed off my running shoes.

He removed his jacket.

I hung it on the coat tree, then added my own. We were already in the third week of September, and weather could be unpredictable.

Tonight was brisk, with a breeze coming off the ocean. The meteorologist predicted rain tomorrow for our game.

That was fine. I didn't mind getting wet. "Uh, do you want something to drink?" Because being a good host was a thing.

"I'll take a glass of water, and then what I want is you. Naked. On the bed."

Part of me wanted to point out that we hadn't even kissed.

The rest of me—led by my very interested cock—pointed out kissing was highly overrated and naked was a very good thing.

I headed to the kitchen, grabbed two bottles of water, and then led him into my bedroom. I handed him a water, placed mine on the nightstand, then made a show of pulling the condoms and lube out of my drawer.

Just in case he might think safe sex wasn't on the agenda for tonight.

My mama raised me to be careful.

As I unbuttoned my jeans, Badarse headed over to the window.

In these older buildings, the windows didn't tend to be floor-to-ceiling.

If I wanted the best perspective, I'd escape to my sliding glass door and my tiny balcony. Just enough space for two loungers.

Just before I let my jeans fall in a heap to the floor, I remembered my cell phone. I extracted it from my back pocket, hooked it up to the charger by my bed, and continued to hastily remove my clothes.

Jeans, underwear, and T-shirt all dropped haphazardly to the floor. Socks yanked off. Then I pulled back my comforter and crawled onto the king bed. With my size, I didn't have much chance at dignity.

Mama always told me Dad had been a big guy and that I'd taken after him. In fact, she reckoned I was even bigger. I never asked about him. A painful divorce when I was three had left her hurting in ways I saw clearer now that I was an adult.

"Uh, do you want me on my front or my back?" I didn't really have a preference. Well, except I kinda liked looking a guy in the eyes when he came. With strangers? I didn't care one way or the other. Not really.

"You comfortable on your front?"

Does he mean because of my size or some psychological thing? "I'm fine that way."

"Great. I'm going to prep you."

My semi plumped nicely at that idea.

"And it's going to be good."

I offered what I thought of as my cocky grin. "I'm counting on it."

Chapter Three

Travis

Marshmallow lying on his front, with his glorious ass sticking in the air, was truly a sight to behold.

Slowly—deliberately—I removed my clothes. Making sure each item made a noise as it landed on his hardwood floor. Well, I put my phone on his chest of drawers, but everything else wound up in a heap on the ground.

He hadn't appeared to mind with his own things. Although maybe he'd just been in a rush.

I like that idea.

After snagging a condom and the bottle of lube, I positioned myself on the bed behind him. I gave myself a couple of tugs and donned the rubber. Then I coated my fingers and started to work him open.

He was tight, which I liked, but slowly—under my gentle ministrations—he began to open for me.

"That's it. Just keep breathing. You like this?" I brushed my finger lightly over his prostate.

He moaned. "Yes, God, that."

I love when they include God *in their pleasure.* Something very naughty about that.

"Please."

Oh, I loved it even more when they begged.

Deciding I'd played enough, I slid my fingers from him.

He groaned.

I slicked up my cock and positioned myself. "You ready?"

He nodded frantically.

I pressed in. Usually, with a stranger, I took things easy. Got to know the guy's body a bit.

Marshmallow's entire being begged to be taken. Like he was made for my cock.

Once fully seated, I withdrew and thrust.

He let out an inarticulate gasp.

"More?"

"Yes." No missing the pleading tone.

So I did what I was best at—drilled him into the mattress.

I thrust, over and over. I pushed him higher and higher. I gave him zero surcease as I gave him everything he clearly wanted.

Chasing my own orgasm was always pleasurable, but I wanted him to come with me. "Jerk yourself."

He stuck his hand under himself and started jerking himself to the punishing rhythm I set.

Please come. Please come. Please come. Sometimes I might come before my partner, but I preferred ensuring he'd had his pleasure first. Being a Dominant, and even on occasion a sadist, was fun. Even more fun was tumbling over when the guy was in the throes of his own orgasm.

He slowed his pace.

"Faster. I want you to come. Like, right now." I injected just the right amount of command into my words.

Which worked because just three tugs later, he came.

Spectacularly.

And as he spasmed around me, my own orgasm took hold. "Thank fuck." I emptied into him, even as he continued to shudder his release.

"Oh my God." His words came in panted breaths.

I grinned. *Nope. I'm not God. But that experience was divine.*

By the time my orgasm waned, I was damn nearly boneless. I slipped from him, and then flopped to the mattress beside him.

He moaned again as he rolled to his side, facing me. He stretched his legs, sighed, then met my gaze. "That was…"

"Yeah."

"And you…?"

"Oh, yeah."

He smiled. "That's good. That's really good." His eyes drifted shut.

Okay. Not really what I expected. Maybe he was one of those guys who went to sleep right after sex. Personally, I preferred to bask a little.

Often, though, the guy just wanted to leave. Or wanted me to leave.

Marshmallow's breathing deepened.

I chose not to be offended. Instead, I congratulated myself for giving him a great orgasm. Slowly, I removed the condom. Then I slid from the bed. I tossed the condom into the trash, pulled the comforter over the guy, put my clothes back on, and slipped from the room.

Man, I could rob him blind and he wouldn't know until he woke up.

I wouldn't, of course, I wasn't that kind of guy. But I worried he might one day hook up with a guy who would take advantage.

After donning my boots, I put on my jacket. I was just about to exit when movement caught my eye.

A black cat lazily strolled down the hallway toward me. Its brown-gold eyes never left mine as it meandered.

"You're just as trusting as he is." I whispered the words, even though the bedroom was on the other side of the condo.

The cat plopped onto its butt and gazed at me. Assessing. Judging.

"I can't stay." Another whisper.

It licked its paw, still staring.

I didn't like the idea of leaving the door unlocked, especially given how soundly Marshmallow slept, but the building had security, this was a pretty safe neighborhood, and I had a sneaking suspicion the cat would gouge out the eyes of any would-be troublemaker.

So I saluted said cat, opened the door, and slid out, leaving the deadbolt unlocked.

The entire ride home, I questioned that decision. Everything from *should I have cleaned him up* to *what harm would it have been to stay the night?*

Answering the first was easy—yes, I should've been more considerate.

The second was a bigger challenge. I didn't stay the night. Guys didn't invite me to. I was more than accustomed to getting on my bike and heading back to my eastside apartment.

As I flew along the Georgia Street viaduct, and worried about stupid city drivers, I considered a longer ride. Along Hastings Street and maybe to the highway. Somewhere I could let go.

Except I didn't have a death wish, and driving at night was even more dangerous than driving during the day.

A friend of mine got taken out a couple of years ago. Fucking pickup truck turned left in front of him, even though the light was green. My friend died on impact and the driver had his license taken away for a couple of years.

Life sucks.

And then you die.

Alone.

Like my mom had.

Which was not a thought I was going to entertain tonight.

I made it home safely, stowed my bike, and headed up to my place. Once inside, I settled with a beer, turned on the television, and tried to settle in.

Ten hours later, I awoke with a crick in my neck and the Saturday-morning news show blaring.

I had no more answers now than I'd had last night.

Chapter Four

Isaiah

"Well, someone got lucky last night." Johnnie grinned.

I surreptitiously glanced around the locker room. *Is he talking about me or is he saying* he *got lucky last night?*

With him, it could go either way.

Johnnie was an oversharer. Truly. The man didn't know how to shut up. And since he got *lucky* several times a week, we all got to hear about his successful conquests.

His word, not mine.

He grinned widely.

I blew out a breath of relief.

He slapped me on the back. "Okay, who's the lucky bloke, and when are you going to introduce us?"

Aw shit. Spoke too soon. "I have no idea what you're talking about."

He grinned—all golden-blond hair, shimmering dark-blue eyes, and a healthy tan from the summer sun. The man was so damn handsome, it hurt to look at him.

I'd had a crush for years as I'd watched the team play. In truth, he was as good-hearted as he was handsome—which made his being straight, and therefore not interested in me—all the more frustrating.

"What lucky bloke?" Roger sauntered into the locker room with a wide grin on his face. He was the opposite of Johnnie—dark hair, dark eyes, and happily married with four kids and a fifth on the way.

Oh, and a wife who should've been due for sainthood. Becca attended every game and often hosted some, or all, of the crew for legendary cookouts in their Burnaby home.

We were a respectful bunch.

For the most part.

"No bloke." We often used the word because Jason bandied it about. And he was from England, so somehow that all made sense.

"Isaiah got lucky last night, and he's not sharing details." Johnnie eyed me. "I guess we can be respectful."

"How's your shoulder?"

He'd bruised it again in the last match. His previous injury was forever haunting him—even more than the head knocks he took.

Rugby was not for the faint of heart.

"It's fine." He rotated it, as if to prove everything was perfect.

I didn't miss the flash in his eyes. Whether pain or relief there wasn't pain, I couldn't be certain. "Okay, so all good to start?"

"Of course."

Roger dropped his bag in front of his cubby. "Me too. Thanks for asking." He winked.

I rolled my eyes.

Somehow he'd managed to get through most of last season without an injury.

I tried to be careful—because Mama was always watching—but I still got knocked around pretty good.

The Toronto team was especially nasty to us. Old rivalry. Because we kept beating them.

Québec's team, based out of Montréal, could also be nasty—but that was because they consistently won when they played us, and they appeared to feel keeping that unbroken record of twelve matches was critical to their self-worth.

Or some shit like that.

Johnnie patted my knee. "You ready?"

I stretched my neck and gave a quick nod. "Yeah." My uniform, though, would provide little protection from the pouring rain. At least the fans in the stands would be covered.

"Mama coming to the game?"

"Nah. She's working the late shift at the hospital." Mama was a nurse who worked at St. Paul's Hospital in downtown Vancouver.

I worried about her—working with some of the most destitute people in the city, including drug addicts and those living in poverty.

She worried about me—because I regularly got knocked around in a sport I loved as much as breathing.

We did okay.

"Gather round." Our coach, Lawrence, beckoned us over. He'd give us another rousing speech about teamwork.

I'd remember that I was lucky to be a fullback on the defensive line, and I'd do my damnedest to keep the other team from scoring. We had a solid offense, great kickers, and a defense to be reckoned with. All that being said, we were fallible. A few times we'd blown leads in games we should've won. Or won fluky games where we hadn't played our best and maybe hadn't deserved the victory.

What will tonight bring?

Why did Badarse leave my bed?

Why did I fall asleep so soon after sex?

That wasn't normal for me. Had I been nervous about today's game? That should've meant I'd stay up worrying instead of falling asleep so quickly, right?

I'd awoken to my alarm at seven with Mamba curled against me and no sign I'd had a visitor the night before.

Oh, except for the used condom in the trashcan.

Johnnie squeezed my arm.

Shit.

No one else was looking at me, though, so clearly I wasn't missing anything critical.

You need to get your head in the game.

Not just because of not wanting to let my team down. No, because inattention on the field could lead to a devastating injury. We didn't wear gear. No padding. Nothing but bodies colliding in bone-crunching ways.

And I'd never been happier.

I'm living my best life.

"Who's going to win?" Lawrence eyed us all.

"Team Orcas," we all shouted in response.

And headed for the field.

Chapter Five

Travis

"You look like your puppy died." Joe handed me another beer. My third.

I'd taken a bus to my favorite bar on Granville Street in Downtown Vancouver. At night, this place was always alive with animated patrons and great music. During the day, it had a couple of televisions going with sports playing.

"Never had a puppy."

"That's too bad." He pointed to my empty plate of nachos, clearly asking if I wanted a refill.

I shook my head. Not now, anyway. If I stayed a few more hours, I just might. I eyed the downpour outside the window. Yeah, no rush to head home.

"I had a dog when I was growing up."

"Yesterday?"

Joe had a young face. What some might call a baby face. He hadn't yet, to my mind, matured enough to even be manning the bar.

He pointed. "Good one. I turned thirty last month."

I blinked.

"Yeah, I know. You should see my great-grandfather. Doesn't look a day over sixty and yet he's ninety-three. Good genes."

I couldn't fathom living to sixty, let alone ninety-three. I spent too much time punishing myself at a very physical job where injuries were rare, but vicious. "That's great news for you. Long life."

He grinned. "Yeah, but I don't want to be a bartender for the rest of my life. I'm dipping my toe into acting. I've got an agent and everything."

"Wow." I knew absolutely nothing about the entertainment industry.

No, that wasn't strictly true. I knew the whole thing was huge up here in Vancouver, and I knew breaking in was super tough.

"You going to be the next Ryan Reynolds?" Hometown boy who had done incredibly well for himself—and insisted on giving back to Canada every chance he got.

"I wouldn't go that far." He leaned closer. "See that group near the back?"

Surreptitiously, I flicked my gaze that way. About fifteen people. "Yeah, okay."

"They're from *Vigilante Justice*. Some cast, some crew, and the producer."

"Okay."

"I would do anything to get a part on that show. Even just a walk-on role."

Slowly, I returned my gaze to him. "I don't watch the show."

Joe's eyes widened. "Oh God, you're missing out. It's amazing. It's about this superhero and his nemesis..."

He continued on about some plot, but I sort of—to my shame—tuned him out. If the people from the show were here, then why not just go over? I was a proponent of taking risks. If I hadn't, I wouldn't have gone home with Marshmallow last night.

I should just call him Mallow. I often gave guys nicknames in my mind. Especially if I hadn't gotten their name. *You could've gotten his name. Hell, you might have even gotten a repeat if you hadn't taken off like the chickenshit you are.*

Sure. But then I'd have had to admit I'd felt differently about him. That last night hadn't been a usual— "Holy shit."

"What?" Joe cocked his head. "You didn't hear a word—"

I pointed to the television. "What the fuck is that?"

He turned for just a moment, then turned back. "That, my friend, is rugby. You've never seen a game before?"

No, I was certain I hadn't.

Yes, I wish I had before now.

Because before me was Mallow, being slapped on the back by a guy in the same turquoise-and-black uniform.

Turquoise had been my mother's favorite color. Otherwise I would've just called it some weird shade of blue or green.

All of a sudden, men from what were clearly opposing sides, all leaned in and made this weird...formation.

"What the fuck is that?"

"A scrum."

"Hey, Joe?" A soft lilting voice came from behind me.

I was too entranced in the show to pay her any mind.

"Yeah, Polly?"

"Valentino would like a rum and Coke."

Joe cleared his throat.

"I'll watch the bar if you want to deliver it to him. Do you have your headshot handy?"

At that, I glanced over. I'd seen Polly around, but she mainly served the tables while Joe or one of the other bartenders kept this part going. I offered her a smile.

She gave one back. "Joe's trying to land a role on the show Valentino produces."

"So he said." I smiled. "I think he'd do well." Truthfully, I didn't know him all that well. I tended to stick to seedier bars on the eastside. But when I wanted something more upscale, I made my way here.

"Okay." Joe prepared the drink.

And his hand shook as he added the rum.

"You going to be okay?" I arched an eyebrow.

"Yeah, of course." He sucked in a breath. "I just have to make certain I don't spill it on him."

"You'll be fine." Again, no reason to be certain of this, but I wished the guy well.

Polly slid in behind the bar.

Joe departed.

My gaze went back to the television.

Apparently hers followed as she sighed. "I love the Orcas. That Roger guy is so hot. Married, though."

"Do you know all the players?"

"Nah. Just the big ones. Roger's a flanker, Isaiah's the fullback, and Johnnie's the hooker."

I sputtered the sip of beer I'd just taken. "The what?"

She pressed a napkin into my hand. "The hooker. Maybe come back one day and I'll tell you what I know. Valentino's group is large enough that I can't take the time."

A shot of the crowd let me know something had happened.

Mallow shook his arms in the air.

I cleared my throat. "And him?"

"Isaiah." She squinted. "I can't remember his last name. I think he's the only one with that name on the team. I'm sure if you look him up, you can learn more about him." She gazed over, but a commercial had come on. "He's a cute one."

I cocked my head.

"Well, you told me you were gay."

"Jesus, I don't remember that."

She shrugged. "I think I was talking about a cute couple I knew. I've met a bunch, especially over the last year. That film crew has acquired a few guys lately. Oh, and a few gals. Elouise Hynes and her wife are here today. Uh...Kelci."

I might've lived under a rock for most of my life, but even I knew who Elouise Hynes was. A Canadian actress who had recently won an Academy Award. I glanced over at the group.

Sure as hell, a woman with wheat-blond hair had her arm around a woman with purple hair.

I turned back to Polly. "And Isaiah's gay?"

She nodded. "One of the first to come out in the Canadian league. Made quite a splash. Not many pro sports athletes are that brave."

Even more for him to have come to the bar last night.

"Uh, thanks Polly." I turned my attention back to the television in time to see a guy ram into another guy who threw the white ball sideways and then he threw it behind him to another guy and on that went for a good minute before someone finally skidded across the line.

Mallow was right there to clap the guy on the back.

The score went up by five.

I rubbed my forehead.

Guess I have a lot to learn.

Except...I hadn't given Mallow my number. And yeah, I knew where he lived. But if I just showed up, would he let me in? If I left a note with the concierge, would Mallow even bother to respond?

You really screwed the pooch when you walked away without a backward glance.

Except I had glanced backward. Last night as I'd fallen asleep and again right now. I was looking back and regretting my hasty retreat.

And fearing it was too late to do anything about it.

Chapter Six

Isaiah

"You make the best sapasui." I gave Mama my winningest smile.

She ruffled my short hair. "You scored the winning goal. So I make your favorite. Seems simple to me."

Given how hard she worked at her day job, it was hardly fair for her to come home and make my favorite meal. She enjoyed spoiling me, though.

And I sort of enjoyed being spoiled...so it all worked out.

"Are you working Thanksgiving?"

She shook her head. "No, but I'm working Christmas."

"That's good of you."

"Well, my baby is all grown up. I figure I can take the extra shifts and let the mothers and fathers be home with their children." She pointed her fork at me. "Will you be okay?"

"Of course. Maybe Johnnie and I can do something."

She narrowed her eyes. "That boy is trouble."

I burst out laughing. "Mama, he's older than I am. And he's never *in trouble*."

"No, trouble just follows him around."

Okay, so he might've gotten a woman pregnant last year.

He'd been prepared to marry her. She'd miscarried and had ended the relationship. He hadn't said anything, but he'd been heartbroken.

I think he'd kind of liked the idea of being a dad.

Despite everything, he'd been prepared to try to make the relationship work. Apparently the woman hadn't felt the same way.

"He's trying."

"He is that." She arched an eyebrow. "But you're sticking to the nice boys, right?"

Mama had figured out I was gay almost before I had. She'd respected my decision not to come out until I'd been in the league a year, though. From age fourteen to twenty-four, I'd hidden who I really was. Not ideal for a young man with raging hormones—but I'd had a larger goal in mind. I wanted to play professional rugby. To me, that meant staying in the closet.

"Nice boys..." I eyed my mother.

"What?" She might've snapped that. Then she waved her fork at me. "Are you going to the bars again?"

"You make it sound like it's a bad thing. I've met some very nice men at those *bars*."

She pursed her lips. "Why don't you try going to the cultural center? Or you could come to church."

A discussion we'd had often. "I don't fit in there, Mama."

"Things are changing." She wrinkled her nose.

On this we'd agreed to disagree. I didn't believe in God or divine intervention.

Mama believed fervently and went to church whenever she could. The community had always taken care of her when she needed help, and she was always happy to give back.

I didn't feel the same kinship.

"So what are you planning for Thanksgiving? I leave for Toronto the next day."

"A feast, of course. Your grandmother is asking when you'll visit her."

Since my grandmother lived thousands of miles away, the comment caught me off guard. "It's not a great time right now—"

She waved me off. "It's never a good time. You're off over Christmas. I'm working. Book a ticket and go home."

Home was somewhere I hadn't been since I was three.

After the divorce, my mother had returned to Canada to work in a care home. Eventually, her nursing credentials, which she'd earned while living in New Zealand, had been recognized and she'd started working at St. Paul's.

I was so damn proud of her

We'd only been back to the island, my father's home, a handful of times. Mostly because of the expense. That, and Mama worked a lot of hours.

I grasped her hand. "I worry about you."

She patted my hand. "I have fifteen more years, and then I can retire."

"Mama, you work in the emergency department. Can't you find somewhere quieter?" On the couple of occasions I'd visited, the place had been organized chaos. Or, that one time, pandemonium.

"You worry too much, and we're off topic."

Oh shit.

"When are you going to bring a nice boy home to meet your mama?"

I closed my eyes, trying to blot out the image of the rough Badarse. I tried not to think about how hard he'd made me come. Or how he'd walked out. "I just haven't met the right man yet. Man, not boy." She knew I had a thing for older guys. "But as soon as I meet someone who might meet your standards, I'll bring him around."

"Harrumph." She grumped. "You think I have high standards."

"You *do* have high standards." I squeezed her hand. "And I love you for it."

As I drove home, I considered her words. Why couldn't I meet a *nice boy* and settle down? I wanted all the things Roger had—a wonderful partner, great kids, and true stability.

Nothing like the life Johnnie lived. I adored him, but didn't want to be like him either.

Which circled me back to Badarse. If I took him at face value, he was just a guy who liked to ride men hard, and then leave them wanting more.

God knew, I wanted more.

More ecstasy.

More intimacy.

More of him...

Instead of heading back to my condo, I turned my car toward the bar I'd been to last night.

Was it really just last night?

Four hours later, after having turned down a couple of *nice* men, I was done.

Okay, maybe nice was wrong. They'd been sexy as hell. And all twinks who clearly wanted to bottom.

No rough-and-tumble guys who wanted to drill me into the mattress.

Give up. You'll never find him. And if he'd wanted a return trip, he would've left his number.

I couldn't argue with that. So I curled up with Mamba and watched the sports recap, only crawling into bed when I couldn't keep my eyes open any longer.

Chapter Seven

Travis

Apparently pouring rain didn't keep away the hometown crowds.

I wore my slicker, heavy boots, and a baseball cap. Theoretically the stadium seating was covered.

In theory.

When the rain pelted sideways in high winds, though, jeans were bound to get soaked. I hadn't moved the entire game because I didn't want my dry ass to get wet.

Other fans gave me a wide berth.

After looking at me, the guy selling hot dogs had scrambled away and not come back.

You're scowling. You're scaring people off. Hell, my scar did a lot of the work. And when I smiled, it always looked a little crooked. So I just didn't bother.

On the field, four guys hauled one guy in the air.

He caught the ball.

And they were off again.

The weather was absolutely not stopping these freaking idiots. I couldn't even imagine how cold and wet they were.

Well, I could. I'd worked some dicey days atop one of Vancouver's tallest skyscrapers. I wore multiple layers of shirts and stripped them off as I sweated through them. Some blazing-hot days, I was ready to strip down to my naked scrawny torso. Other days, like today, I needed every ounce of body heat I could summon.

The ball passed back and forth between four Orca players as they made their way down the field, and the next thing I knew, Mallow was skidding across the line with one arm stuck out and the ball tightly gripped under the other.

The crowd roared.

Even I jumped out of my seat and pumped my arm in the air.

The players all slapped each other on the backs.

As I settled back into my seat, a young girl caught my eye.

She drew her finger down her face, exactly mirroring my scar. Then she pulled her mouth into a massive grin.

I tried for a scowl. I really did. When confronted with her unrelenting grin, however, I couldn't help but smile back. Without a doubt, mine would be crooked, but I gave it a try.

"Sweetheart, what are you doing?" The blond woman next to the girl gazed between her daughter and me. Or at least I assumed they were mother and daughter. The woman met my eye. "I'm so sorry."

I shook my head. "No, it's okay." I tried to continue to smile. "Your daughter is very sweet." I sought the right word. "Charming."

She rolled her eyes. "My daughter is headstrong—much like her father." The woman stuck out her hand. "Becca. My lug is the blind-side flanker, Roger. And this," she pressed a hand to her daughter's shoulder, "Is Cassandra. The bane of my existence."

Inwardly I winced even as I shook her hand.

Cassandra rolled her eyes. "You know you love me."

The crowd emitted another roar.

"Oh, sorry." I pointed to the field. "I made you miss some of the game."

Becca waved me off. "I've been doing this a long time." She pressed her hand to what I now saw was a distended belly. "Number five. Going to be a kicker like his father."

"And me." Cassandra grinned. "I'm going to play rugby. You know, they have an Olympic women's team. Ten years? I'm on it."

Holy crap. "That's...amazing."

"What's your name?"

"Uh...Travis." *Because Badarse isn't likely to go over well. On second thought, I think feisty Cassandra would laugh.*

Cassandra stuck out her hand. "I'm Cassandra. Not Cassie." She eyed me.

"Not Cassie." I said the words with true solemnity. Somehow I got the feeling this pint-sized child would tear a strip off me if I got it wrong. She truly appeared fearless.

"Are you here to see someone or just to catch the game?" Becca tipped her raincoat back so the gathering moisture trickled down the hood toward her back.

A reminder the rain was soaking us.

"Uh..." *Oh fuck it.* "I've met the, uh, fullback?"

Her face broke into a big grin.

Before she could respond, Cassandra whooped. "You know Uncle Isaiah? How cool is that? Are you coming to meet him after the game?"

"Uh..." Truthfully, I hadn't thought that far in advance. I'd just...shown up without a plan.

"Of course he's coming with us." Becca offered a brilliant smile.

"Yeah, I guess so."

Another roar from the crowd.

Becca beckoned to the empty chair next to Cassandra. "I was supposed to bring my son, Tristan, but he's got a cold. I didn't have time to find anyone else. Our seats have a bit more protection from the rain."

The difference was infinitesimal, but the offer meant everything.

I moved and sat next to Cassandra as she and Becca had retaken their seats.

Becca offered me a smile over Cassandra's head. "Nice to meet you."

"Yeah, you too."

Chapter Eight

Isaiah

"Great game." Johnnie slapped me on the back. "I didn't think you were going to make it."

I rolled my shoulder.

And tried not to wince. "Yeah, he got me good."

"Plenty of ice tonight."

"Yeah, that's what Francine suggested."

Our trainer was, frankly, one of the best in the league.

I glanced over to Jason. "How's the head?" He'd taken a hell of a knock.

"Went through the concussion protocol, and I'm fine. Really, nothing to worry about."

Except head injuries and concussions were a real concern in our lives. Without any padding, if the player's head hit the ground, nothing would cushion the fall. Take an elbow or knee to it as well, and... Yeah, we'd all been through concussion protocol.

"Oh, Becca brought Cassandra to the game." Roger grinned. "So I'm going to pass on the celebration."

Johnnie slapped Roger on the back, much as he had with me. "You're not going to bring them?"

"You think you can refrain from swearing in front of my eleven-year-old impressionable and stubborn daughter?"

"Nothing she won't hear once she starts playing." Johnnie's eyes shone. "Our little girl, all grown up."

Roger smacked him on the chest. "You had nothing to do with her upbringing, thank God. And you're not going to get near her now. Sure, she's old enough to hear swear words. She's also old enough to take them home. You know what Tristan's like—parrots every god-damn thing he hears. Linus and Evelyn will hear everything."

Johnnie laughed uproariously. "What exactly did you say when you hit your thumb with the hammer when we were hanging that family portrait and, to commemorate the occasion, your entire family was watching?"

My ears perked. I hadn't heard this story.

"I might've..." Roger winced.

"Said *Jesus Fucking Christ*?" Another laugh from Johnnie.

Oh dear.

"Yes, my dearly beloved grandmother-in-law would've smited me on the spot." My friend rubbed his forehead. "I'm still not certain Becca's forgiven me for that transgression."

"Well, at least you don't have an *actual* parrot." I grinned.

Johnnie and Roger groaned.

Jason's parrot was legendary. Our teammate liked to bring Walter to every gathering he could get away with. Little fucking bird had the biggest potty mouth of all of us.

"I'm not coming tonight." Roger jutted his chin. "I have standards. You two don't meet them."

I laughed. "Oh my God, you did not just say that."

"Daddy!" Cassandra darted toward us as we made our way to the greeting area.

Roger scooped her into his arms. "Hey, bug."

"Harrumph."

We all chuckled.

Cassandra was growing up so damn fast.

I want that. I want someone to greet me with that much enthusiasm. Even if I can't have a kid, a partner would be nice—

"Isaiah!" Becca called my name and waved me over.

I pulled her into a hug, grateful for her evident happiness to see me. Not exactly the usual, but she always gave everyone hugs. I figured Johnnie would be next—along with some good old-fashioned teasing.

"You big lug." She smacked my arm.

I stepped out of her embrace.

She pointed behind her.

Badarse stood there with the most uncertain look on his face.

Clearly, he dreaded my reaction. *Well, yeah, because holy shit, he's here...*

"Nice to see you again." Was I supposed to shake hands? Offer a hug? Surely a kiss was out of the question.

"Hello, Mallow."

I cocked my head. "Uh, that's not my name." I stepped closer, hopefully out of Becca's hearing. "It's Isaiah."

He offered me a beautiful lopsided grin. "You'll always be marshmallow to me."

"Hey, who are you?" Johnnie stepped up beside me. "This area's restricted."

"Yeah, you should be going." Roger came up on my other flank.

"He's with me." Becca pushed her way past all of us and linked arms with Badarse. "Travis joined me for the game. Cassandra and I decided we wanted him to join us." She eyed me. "I'm certain Isaiah doesn't mind."

Oh my God, the woman was a firebrand. Even if I didn't want to see Badarse—Travis—again, I wouldn't dare speak up against Becca.

"No, I'm so glad you brought him." I met Badarse's gaze. "I didn't realize you were a rugby fan."

He held my gaze. "I'm an Isaiah fan."

Holy hell.

Johnnie roared with laughter. "Oh wow, Isaiah has a boyfriend."

"We didn't—"

"I'm not—"

Badarse and I started to speak at the same time and then we stopped at the same time.

I turned to Johnnie. "Fuck off, okay? He's my...friend."

Badarse leaned over and whispered, "Hey, Mallow. Don't go around telling people I have friends. It's bad for my image." He pulled back and met my gaze. "Take me home... and teach me about rugby."

I blinked. "What?" I swallowed. "Can you repeat that?"

"I wanna learn about rugby."

"Why?" He'd come to the game and sat next to Cassandra and Becca. Which I still couldn't believe. If Cassandra hadn't taught him about the game, then what had they discussed? The thought made me slightly queasy.

"I dunno." He offered that adorable smile again. "Let's give it a shot."

"You like me?" Processing this was proving difficult because my own emotions swirled. A week ago, he'd walked out on me. Now, he stood before me and wanted...more.

I was intrigued.

"Fuck off. You're a mallow... just fucking teach me about rugby so next time I come to your game I can understand what you're doing out there..."

"Just kiss him already." Johnnie joined us, standing where he could put his hands on both our backs and try to squeeze us together.

Badarse and I were strong enough that Johnnie had to really strain.

In the end, I moved forward first.

My companion, of sorts, moved closer as well.

Becca appeared on the other side and stuck her arm between us, wagging her finger at Johnnie. "You leave them alone. If they want to kiss, then they'll kiss. If they want to be left in peace, then we'll damn well leave them in peace."

Then, as if this wasn't all crazy enough, Cassandra wormed her way between Badarse and me. She glared at Johnnie. "You need to be respectful."

My teammate appeared immediately contrite, as he bowed his head a bit.

"Consent is important." She put her hands on her hips. "They have to give permission first."

Jesus, we're getting a lecture from an eleven-year-old who is apparently smarter than all of us.

"You're right." Johnnie stood taller. "I apologize."

"You'd better." She held the serious expression for another moment before glancing up at me. She gestured to Badarse with her chin. "I like him."

I held her gaze for a moment longer before meeting his eyes. "I think I might like him too." Especially if he was willing to learn about rugby.

Becca grabbed my hand. "Why don't we head out for a quiet dinner together?" She eyed the gaggle of guys hanging with wives, girlfriends, or just by themselves. The rowdy bunch.

I usually went with them, but I wasn't a drinker and didn't always fit in. I met Becca's gaze. "I'd be up for that." Then I met Badarse's eyes. "You? Or do you want—"

"I want." He held my gaze with those mesmerizing blue eyes. "I'd really like."

Not knowing what was coming next, but willing to give it a shot, I held out my hand. "Let's go."

Cassandra clapped, then hugged Johnnie around the waist. "You're coming too, right Uncle Johnnie?"

For a moment, he looked longingly over at the other guys who were heading out to our favorite pub. He ruffled Cassandra's hair—in a way he knew drove her nuts. "Of course." He glanced at me. "I wouldn't miss this for the world."

Chapter Nine

Travis

*C*an an eleven-year-old be a matchmaker?

That question swirled in my mind as I sat across from Mallow at Brown's Social House. Fortunately, the place was somewhere between dive bar and five-star dining. Perhaps a little closer to the latter, but I'd survive. Everyone else wore jeans with various types of footwear. We'd all shed our outerwear, and now I was pleased I'd put on a clean henley.

Dodge, my friend at work, claimed the color matched my eyes.

Well, our coworker, Annabelle, had pointed it out, and Dodge repeated it, so that meant two people liked it.

Right?

I just didn't know.

Cassandra sat primly next to me and pointed to the menu. "They really do make amazing burgers, but their bowls are exceptional."

Exceptional? I wasn't certain I'd ever used that word in my life.

"Bowls?

"The Southwest Rice Bowl is good. I also like the Dragon Bowl."

I quickly scanned the menu. Black beans. Uh, no. My digestive system didn't do well with black beans—something I'd learned the hard way. "How are the fish and chips?" Something to be said for going simple.

"They're good." Mallow offered a shy smile. "So's the French Dip. Have whatever you like. My treat."

Cassandra sighed. "Almost like a date."

I nearly scowled, but somehow managed not to. "I can pay my own way." Because I could. This place wasn't astronomical in price. I could fit it into the budget.

"I'm certain you can." Mallow tapped his shoe to my boots. "But I want to thank you for coming to the game and getting soaking wet."

He wasn't wrong. My damp jeans clung uncomfortably to my thighs and a bit of my neck had gotten wet when I'd removed my slicker. My own fault—not paying attention. Nope, I'd been watching a certain fullback removing his jacket and showing off nice muscles beneath his tight T-shirt. "Yeah, okay. This time."

Cassandra giggled. "That means you're going out again."

Becca turned to her daughter. "Are you meddling?"

"You mean like when I told Uncle Jason about the woman with the—"

"Cassandra." Becca hissed the word under her breath, but still audible to said young woman as well as Mallow and me.

She just shrugged. "I thought you said we're supposed to be honest."

Becca sighed. "There is such a thing as too much honesty."

Cassandra arched an eyebrow delicately.

Jesus, I can't even do that. Now I'm jealous of a child. Well, she clearly verged on teenager hood, and I would've pegged her as slightly older. But then I knew nothing about kids.

"What are you having?" Mallow met Cassandra's stare with one of his own. Clearly he was either braver than me or had done this before. Or needed his head examined. I wasn't certain staring down that young woman was such a good idea. That being said, she could likely smell blood in the water.

"Tiki Tuna Poke Bowl." She closed her menu.

I blinked.

"Some of it will come home in a container." Becca smiled. "She doesn't eat all of it."

"Harumph." Cassandra looked displeased, with a little furrow between her eyebrows. "I'm a growing girl." She straightened and nodded to me. "I'm training."

I blinked.

"I do track and field. I'm a runner. Building up speed and agility." She crossed her arms. "I wish we had rugby at my school."

"Uh...what grade are you in?"

"Seventh."

I tried to do the math on that.

"I skipped a grade. School's so boring." More pouting.

Becca sighed. "Cassandra is...advanced. The school decided she might get up to less mischief if she skipped third grade entirely."

"Didn't miss it." She ran her hand through her short hair. "I can't wait to get to high school."

I cleared my throat. "Yeah, I had the same attitude." I considered my next words carefully. "I didn't take school seriously. I was dumb anyway, so why bother?"

Isaiah tapped my foot with his.

"I got into trouble with the cops. All juvie stuff, but I wound up dropping out. I dicked around—pardon."

Becca waved me off.

"Doing nothing good, I mean." I winced. "Then my mom got sick, and I had to take care of us. I got a job working in a fabricating plant. I was making good money, but the shop wasn't so good about safety." I gestured to my face. "That was me being inattentive and them not having proper safety protocols." I blinked several times. "I was in the hospital for two weeks and when I got out, I had to take my mom right back there. She died a month later."

Another brush of his foot.

Cassandra frowned.

"Sorry, too blunt."

Becca offered a small smile. "Cassandra's grandmother—Roger's mother—passed away last year after a brief illness. We didn't shield her."

"I miss Grannie. Do you miss your mom?"

Slowly, I nodded. "Yeah, I really do. I wasn't the kid she thought I should be and by the time I tried to grow up, she was gone." I scratched my chin. "But I decided I'd do better. Not even a speeding ticket in twenty years. I work hard, pay my taxes, and stay out of trouble." I pointed to my face. "But people see me a certain way and have certain expectations. Some of those I can meet, and some I can't." I glanced quickly over at Isaiah.

His dark-brown eyes shone. "You'll always meet mine."

He whispered the words, and I strained to hear them over the din of the restaurant.

"I don't care what people look like." Cassandra fingered her menu. "Like, it's what inside that counts." She nudged her dad. "At least that's what he says."

Roger, who had been in a deep conversation with Johnnie, turned his attention to his daughter. "Sorry, sweetheart, we were discussing scrum strategies."

She perked up at that.

"Cassandra was just explaining how someone's outward appearance doesn't matter." Becca closed her menu. "And how it's what's on the inside that counts."

Roger caught my gaze. Slowly, he nodded. "Cassandra's got a good head on her shoulders." He met my gaze. "You're...not what we expected."

Johnnie nodded.

Isaiah coughed.

I shot a glance his way.

He mouthed *later*.

I nodded—truly curious, but also aware small ears were probably the most likely to pick up on nuance that might just go right over my head.

At that moment, the server arrived to take our orders. On a whim, I ordered the steak. I certainly had the funds to take Isaiah out for a nice dinner when we could be alone.

All through dinner, he kept tapping my foot.

I regretted we hadn't sat next to each other so I could press a hand to his thigh.

Unsurprisingly, Cassandra had commanded the seating arrangements.

Much to everyone's amusement.

Dinner turned into dessert where I tried something decadent with Oreos. Who knew a simple cookie could be turned into something so tasty?

Isaiah, Cassandra, Johnnie, and Roger discussed the game in quite some depth.

I did my best to follow. I really did.

In the end, Becca engaged me in a discussion about what I enjoyed most about my job working steel fifty stories above the ground.

Isaiah's focus appeared split between the two conversations, although he left me to my conversation with the charming woman.

I encouraged her to talk about motherhood—a discussion I rarely got to partake in. Most of the guys I worked with, even if they were fathers, didn't share the intricacies of raising four children and being over-the-moon excited about the prospect of adding a fifth. Oh, and having a husband who traveled often. I'd assumed Cassandra would be roped into helping—and she was, on occasion—but Becca's mother-in-law lived with them and, apparently, loved grandmothering.

Again, I might've thought that would be intrusive, but Becca's glowing words made it clear her affection was true.

I loved it.

In the end, the hour was late by the time we called it quits.

Johnnie drove away in his beater car.

Roger, Cassandra, and Becca took off in their minivan.

I wondered how they could fit all those kids in that thing. I supposed there was a way.

"Are you coming home with me?" Isaiah snagged my hand.

"Are you inviting me?"

"Only if you promise not to leave me before saying goodbye." His eyes flashed hurt.

"I...most guys don't want me to stay the night."

"I'd like to think I'm not *most guys*."

I chuckled. "No, you're definitely not." I pressed my hand to his chest. "Yes, Mallow, I'll come home with you."

He grinned. "You know the way. My gate code is 2704."

Four digits I could remember—despite how my heart rate increased and the tightening in my jeans.

The night drizzle continued. "I'm going to be a little wet."

"Oh, I plan to make you a lot...uh..." His scrunched his forehead in an absolutely adorable way. "I don't think I got that right."

I chuckled. "And yet I knew what you meant."

Slowly, he ducked his head. He released my hand, then cupped my cheeks.

Oh my God, he's going to kiss me. I don't kiss. One of few rules I had. Kissing was an intimacy I didn't dare enjoy with anyone. Lest my heart get broken. Yet my eyes drifted shut as he pressed his lips to mine. *I'm a goner.*

Chapter Ten

Isaiah

A nticipation thrummed through me as I drove home.

I kept Badarse in my rearview mirror as I approached my building. Giving him the code had only been for if we got separated. If he was close enough, I could just use my remote for both of us.

We were close enough.

Every time I'd tapped his foot tonight, that closeness had, for me at least, increased. I couldn't be certain about him. He played his cards very close to the vest. He let little through.

Except for moments when he'd let his guard down. When talking to Becca. When sharing some dark parts of his life with Cassandra.

Like when he'd kissed me.

Well, kissed me back.

I hit the remote for the garage.

As I cycled quickly through the evening in my mind, his conversation with Cassandra kept coming to the fore. His brutal honesty.

I understood why he'd done it. He saw his life as a cautionary tale. And, right now, Cassandra was on an incredible trajectory. But things could change in a heartbeat. People died. Accidents happened. Hearts got broken. Those things could lead someone down a dark path.

Badarse was proof one could come out the other side. Yes, with scars, tattoos, and all kinds of other visible examples of pain. But a survivor nonetheless.

I respected him all the more for that.

After exiting my car, I made my way over to him. Without preamble, I snagged him around the waist, and drew him toward me.

He came willingly. Pliantly.

I kissed him. No gentle brushing of lips this time. No this was tongues entwining. This was grinding against each other. This was pure passion. I didn't give a flying fuck if I got hard in my jeans. We only had a short elevator ride up, and then we could carry this sexual tension to its logical conclusion. I wanted him. He clearly wanted me. The rest was just mechanics, positions, and orgasms.

He pulled away first.

I gazed into his lust-filled blue eyes. "What do I call you? Travis or Badarse?"

Those eyes flickered with something I couldn't quite identify. If I had to guess, though, I would've said pain.

"You can call me whatever you like."

"What do your friends call you?" I wanted to ask what his lovers called him, but that felt way too personal a question. And, perhaps, something I didn't want the answer to.

He cleared his throat. "I, uh, don't have a lot of friends."

I ached an eyebrow.

"Well, okay. The mate who nicknamed me was a bit of a friend. So yeah, Badarse has sentimental meaning. My buddy Dodge, who is close to a friend, calls me Trav. I don't really like that, but I'd never say that to him."

"Is there a story behind the name Dodge?"

He grinned. "You bet. But we'll save that for another time."

"Yeah, okay." I tipped his chin so our eyes met. "You didn't answer my question. Badarse, Trav, or Travis?" I hissed that *s* just a little bit.

He pressed his erect cock against my hip. "No one's called me that since my mother."

"Does that make you sad, or—"

"I like it." He blinked. "Badarse is the guy who goes up towers for a living—risking his life. Trav is the guy who hangs out with his—" He cleared his throat. "—friend, Dodge. But Travis is who I could've been. If I hadn't fucked up."

I pressed my finger to his lips. "If you'd fucked up, then we never would've met each other." I sought the right words. "I'll bet your mother would be proud of the man you've become. You turned your life around. Nothing would've prevented her death. But you could've continued down that dangerous and likely deadly path. Or you could've chosen the right way. You did that."

"You make it sound almost religious. Like some divine intervention or shit."

Slowly, I shook my head. "No, that's my mother. I'm more pragmatic. I think human beings have free will and that everything is not predestined. That we choose our paths. And yeah, sometimes we fucking get it wrong. But we can own that and move forward or we can sit and wallow in the shit. I'm for team Moving Forward."

He laughed. "I love your attitude. Okay, I think we've had enough baring of our souls for one night." He picked at his jeans. "You have a dryer? Or can I hang them up somewhere?"

If he hung them up, he'd have to stay longer. Right? "I have a dryer. I avoid using it when I can. I like saving money."

He grinned. "Also an environmentalist?"

I furrowed my brow as if considering before breaking into a huge grin. "Yeah. I like that you get it."

"I get you." He pressed a hand to my chest. "Now, I believe I have plans for you. They involve you. Naked. On your bed. Facing me."

Again, something flashed in his eyes.

My gut reaction, which had no logic but still held, was he didn't fuck many guys facing them. No, he'd likely gone for impersonal.

Whereas I'd done it both ways. I'd had some long-term relationships and would even own I wish one or two of them had lasted. Alas, they hadn't. But if they had, I wouldn't have been in the bar last Friday, and I certainly wouldn't be standing here with this loveable man on a Saturday night. I snagged his hand. "Come."

"Oh, I intend to." He grinned wickedly.

When he did that, I barely noticed his scar. No, I was too entranced by the inherent gentleness that appeared when he let his guard down.

The ride up in the elevator proved an exercise in patience.

Of which I had very little

Still, we stumbled into my condo, and I managed to lock the door. He cupped my crotch.

I moaned as I nuzzled behind his ear. He smelled like the earth. Like the smell I got when I skidded into the grass with a ball tucked under my arm. Which made absolutely no sense...but I'd take it as a sign.

In return, I snagged his ass. Then pulled back. "You're damp."

"Yeah."

"You can drape your jeans over a stool in the kitchen, or you can toss them into the dryer." I held my breath.

He nipped at my chin. "Better to be environmental and cheap, right?"

I exposed my throat. "Oh hell, yes."

He chuckled. He removed his boots, then headed toward the kitchen.

I toed off my running shoes, then made my way to the bathroom.

Mamba followed me with an indignant meow.

"You've been fed."

She glared.

"You're going to be good tonight. I'm about to get lucky. So, like, go play with your stuffed mouse with catnip."

She didn't look impressed.

I gave her a scritch, then shooed her out of the room. "Mamba's a good cat." I tossed that out for Travis, belatedly realizing me might not even know I had a cat.

Oops.

Still, I was in a hurry. A quick piss and a glance in the mirror had me smiling. *I'm going to get laid again. Oh wow.* I'd thought after he'd left last weekend that we were done. Seeing him this afternoon had knocked me sideways.

Thank God Cassandra's so bossy.

I'd been struggling for words.

She'd made certain Travis agreed to come to dinner.

Travis.

I liked his name. I liked that no one ever called him that. I liked that, in essence, he was gifting me with something precious—a piece of himself that he never shared with anyone.

With a last look in the mirror, I headed into the bedroom.

No sight of Travis.

But he'd made his expectations very clear. Naked. Middle of the bed. So I snagged lube and a string of condoms from the nightstand. Then I stripped out of my T-shirt, jeans, socks, and briefs.

Chilled air hit my nether regions, but my hard-on didn't diminish much. After I'd pissed—and as I'd begun the ramp up of anticipation toward this moment—that erection had returned full force.

The water running in the bathroom propelled me into action. I closed the bedroom door, thereby keeping a very curious cat in the living room with her expensive cat tree and many toys. I yanked down the comforter and top sheet, then crawled onto the bed. I put a pillow at the center of the bed, then laid my head on it. With one arm bent behind my head, I stroked my cock leisurely. I swiped my finger across the slit, then rubbed the bead of precum into the crown.

My shaft pulsed.

Travis sauntered into the room.

For the first time, I was truly able to look without fear. Without worrying about my gaze.

He was beautiful. All pale skin, ink, and plenty of body hair. He had a nice pelt on his chest that arrowed down his abdomen to his happy trail. His pubes were a shade darker than the rest of his hair, and his legs were covered. So different from me as I barely had a trace of hair. I'd felt less than a man growing up. When I'd hit puberty with my friends and they'd all matured and I'd lagged behind. Had never really caught up.

Except in size.

He cocked his head.

"It's the ink." Because I wasn't going to mention the inadequacies I'd felt growing up.

That and his ink was truly magnificent. A dragon shooting fire across his chest. A spider web crawling up his neck. The lightning down his cheek.

Was Cassandra as fascinated as I am? She just seemed to accept him as he was. All my friends had. Which I appreciated more than anything I might've been able to express.

"Like what you see?"

"Oh, for sure. I'm just surprised you don't have ink on your legs."

He grinned. "In time. I haven't found a design I like enough to shave and subject myself to that pain. I'm super sensitive to it. Which is ironic, given I push my body to the limit every day I go up a tower."

I wasn't certain I liked the idea of him putting his life on the line every day. But I couldn't remember hearing of any construction person falling to their death, so he must've been relatively safe.

Although I might google statistics later.

"I'm looking forward to using some of that physical limit with me."

He stroked his cock.

His arms were plenty muscular while the rest of him was...smaller. Almost out of proportion. But damn, he looked fine to me.

I spread my legs.

He grinned and made his way over to the bed. "I'm going to make you scream. Will the neighbors be bothered?"

I shook my head. "Solid construction with good soundproofing. One of the reasons I was happy to buy the place."

"It does look sturdy." He let his gaze wander up and down my body with a leisure that made me shiver. "You look pretty sturdy as well."

"Come over here and find out."

He grinned, then crawled onto the mattress and then, in one long fluid movement, placed his body over mine.

Our cocks brushed.

Mine jumped at the contact.

He dove in for a kiss.

I grasped his cheeks and held on tight as I pulled him closer. Then I ran one hand down his flank. I cupped his ass and squeezed.

He moaned, then pulled back from the kiss. "That. I want more of that."

I gazed into his eyes—darker because they were only illuminated by my bedside lamp. "So do I."

He snagged the lube and condom. Then he scooted back so he could position himself between my legs. He rolled on the condom, then poured lube onto his fingers.

I grinned. I didn't mind prepping myself, but the intimacy of someone else doing it always warmed my heart just that little bit. I spread my legs farther apart, giving him unfettered access.

His matching grin made my spirit soar.

He slid his index finger in.

"Oh, you can do better than that."

After he cocked his head, he slid a second finger in.

"Better." Said on a sigh.

He scissored as he sank deeper. "You like this?"

"Yeah."

His finger brushed my prostate.

My cock jumped, leaking a drop of precum.

He leaned over to lick it off. "Yum. One of these days, I'm going to give you a blow job and it'll rock your world."

"We've got all night." I grinned, yet felt the strain behind my words. *Don't push too hard.*

"You're right. We do." He chuckled. "You're young. I bet you have a short refractory period."

I squinted.

"You get hard again quickly."

"If I'm stimulated, then sure."

"Right. Well, I'm not twenty anymore."

"I'm twenty-four."

"And I'm forty and you just made my point."

He brushed his finger against my prostate again, and I gritted my teeth. "Keep that up and this will be over too soon."

"Oh, you're that sensitive?"

"You better believe it." I gripped my hair. "I need to come. But I want you in me."

Slowly, he withdrew his fingers.

I whined. Yep, actually whined.

He slicked his cock and then moved over me. "You ready?"

"Fuck yes. Oh God, please."

"You're a treasure." His eyes shone. "Don't ever forget that, eh?"

Before I could respond, he pressed against my hole.

I relaxed.

He breached me with relative ease, then slid in.

I continued to breathe through the sting, the burn, and then the relief.

A week. We'd only been apart eight days. And yet it felt like a lifetime. Because this was where he was meant to be. In my bed. In my arms.

This feeling made less than no sense, but Mama taught me to go with my gut, and my gut said to hold on to this man and never let go. "Now."

"Yeah, you bet." He withdrew almost to the tip, then thrust back in.

I accepted him. I grasped his back to urge him closer. I nearly asked him to stay like this forever. Instead, I just nipped his neck.

He continued to thrust. Harder and harder. Faster and faster.

Then he took my shaft in his hand. Somehow, his rhythm never faltered as he started jacking me to the brutal tempo he set.

I gripped his sweat-slicked back and held on for the ride as he pushed me higher and higher. "Jesus, I'm going to come. Travis, please—"

"Come. Come, Mallow, okay? You come and then I can—"

I came. Hard. Breathlessly. My vision narrowed as my body soared. Right above the city. I was in the clouds with him on that construction tower—looking down at all the ant people in the streets. Feeling a lightness of being I'd never experienced before. *He did this. He gave you this gift.*

"Oh, thank fuck." He arched his head back as he roared his release.

I stroked my hand up and down his neck, marveling at his trust in me.

Then, without warning, he collapsed on me.

"Oof."

"Sorry." He tried to rise, only succeeding in pressing his hand to my belly.

I swiftly moved the hand away and brought it to my lips, pressing a kiss to the knuckles. "I'm not sorry." I held him close to me.

His flaccid cock slowly slid from me.

I mourned the loss of intimacy. *Yeah, but having him in my arms is so much better. I can hold on and make sure he doesn't leave.* "That was…"

"Yeah."

"And you…?"

"Fuck, yes."

"Oh, well, that's good."

I blinked several times, fighting to keep my eyes open. *Fucking hell. Why do I always fall asleep right after sex?* I'd meant to ask the guys about this, but I hadn't dared. Roger might not make fun of me, but Johnnie would.

"Rest, Mallow. I've got you." He pressed a kiss to my chest. "I'm not going anywhere.

I believed him.

So I closed my eyes and let go.

Chapter Eleven

Travis

I awoke to the distinctive smell of coffee and bacon. The way every good Canadian should, as far as I was concerned.

Orienting myself took mere moments as Mallow's firm mattress cuddled my rumpled self. With a cat wrapped around the top of my head, gently kneading my scalp. As long as she didn't pull my hair, I had no plan to dislodge her. Letting sleeping dogs lie and all that. Cats, dogs...what difference did that matter?

Memories of the previous night flooded back. The blow jobs. The fucking.

I hesitated.

Okay, maybe not.

Well, the first time we'd come together, it'd been violent in all the good ways. He'd implied he wanted me to drill him into the mattress—which I'd happily done.

After that—our second and third joinings—had been tender. Almost magical in a way I'd never encountered before. He'd wanted gentle. Whether he'd actually said those words, or I'd just interpreted them, I couldn't be certain. But he'd wanted something more than pure fucking.

And I'd willingly given it to him. Hell, I'd do anything he asked.

Plus we'd exchanged blow jobs.

Had to say, the man had a talented mouth.

Man?

Lover?

So much shifted last night. I hadn't felt like a guy who abused his body all day long and who sat with heating pads at night. I didn't feel nearly over the hill. Knowing, if I took care of myself, I could have a good long life didn't change the fact some days I felt old. Decrepit. Needing to find more energy.

And wow, my refractory period last night had been a fraction of what it normally was.

One look from Mallow—one simple crooked finger—and I'd been ready to go again. Anything to please him. Anything to bring him pleasure. Anything to enjoy him over and over. My pleasure, as it did with all my partners, took second place. He, whomever he was, needed to come first. I'd done selfish in my teens and early twenties.

After Mom's death, I'd taken a hard look at myself in the mirror—scar, tattoos, and all—and decided I'd be more considerate. I'd try harder. I'd find a way to be a better person.

Despite everything, I wanted to believe I had.

That she'd be proud of the man I'd become.

The look Cassandra had given me last night, as I'd relayed those tough years, assured me she understood. Perhaps in the way only an innocent, yet knowledgeable, child could. Not with pity, but with compassion. She'd understood why I'd shared the story. Why I told anyone who would listen.

I didn't want them taking the same path I had. If one young person chose better, then my life would've been worth it. The pain would've been worth it.

"Oh, you're awake."

Mallow's gentle voice pulled me from my musings. From the inner turmoil I so often faced.

"May I bring you breakfast in bed?" He offered a shy and charming smile.

I winced. "I have to pee."

"Then you can crawl back into bed. I haven't had my fill of you yet."

Last night, in the near-darkness of this room, I hadn't hesitated.

His lamp's illumination barely lit the space. And eventually we'd turned it off. Although fumbling with condoms in the dark had been fun, I felt less confident now. He could see me. All of me. Even with his blinds closed, a lot of light filled the room. *No hiding in the shadows.* One of the reasons I chose dark bars and why I kept my apartment so shrouded. If guys couldn't see me properly, maybe that made it easier for them.

"Hey." He advanced quickly to my side, sitting by the bed and grasping my hand. "Whatever you're thinking, I want you to stop."

I blinked.

Gently, he extricated Mamba from her grasp of my hair. He put her on the floor.

She meowed her displeasure, but still headed out to the living room.

"I can see it. In your eyes. You're hurting. I don't know why, and I don't have the right to ask, but I want to take away that pain. If I don't miss the mark, we had a pretty good time last night."

"We did."

"Then why not continue today? I know you don't work, and I'm completely free. I want to watch the replay of last night's game—"

"And teach me rugby?"

He grinned wickedly. "Among other things. I'm a very good instructor and big on positive reinforcement." He squeezed my hand. "What were you thinking about?"

"You don't want to know."

"I wouldn't have asked if I hadn't wanted to know. The truth is I want to know everything about you. Your past, your present, your dreams for the future...all of it."

I snickered. "You don't want to know my dreams for the future, Mallow. Because I don't have any. Well, staying alive would be good. Retiring with a bit of money in the bank twenty years from now would be okay as well."

"Those are great dreams." He telegraphed his movement as he raised his hand to my cheek.

Slowly, I nodded.

He stroked his hand down my cheek.

I nearly broke on the spot. No one—absolutely no one—had ever touched my face. It just didn't happen. Even if people weren't repulsed, they would never dare.

"Do you...?" He cleared his throat, even as he continued to caress me.

"Do I what?" I closed my eyes and leaned into his touch.

The bed shifted as he moved closer.

I leaned in. Where I expected a kiss, though, he pressed his lips to the scar.

Then, as the pain in my chest expanded to the point where I almost couldn't take anymore, he pulled me into a bear hug.

Into a Mallow hug.

The big bear who was just a teddy bear inside.

We stayed that way for a long time.

Finally, I opened my eyes and pulled back. "What were you going to ask?"

"Have you..." He cleared his throat. "I don't want you to think I'm not incredibly respectful and in awe of what—"

"Just spit it out."

"Do you want...I don't know...a safer job? Somewhere you're not putting your life at risk every day?"

I bit my lip.

"Say it. I promise I won't judge."

"Yeah..." I drew in a deep breath and let it out. "What I didn't tell Cassandra is I eventually went back and earned my high school diploma. And I've even taken a few construction-management courses."

"Which would lead to...?" His excited expression couldn't be overstated.

"Like, I dunno. Maybe a foreman's job. Or an assistant something. I'm learning how to read plans and shit."

"That's...that's amazing." His dark-brown eyes softened. "I mean, I care about you anyway, you get that, right?"

I frowned.

"Just...I don't want you to think that I don't respect what you do—because I totally respect what you do."

"Yeah, okay. I get it." And I did. He would be happier if I wasn't doing such a dangerous job. "Foreman is a tough job."

"Then who better to do it? Someone who knows what the men are going through?"

"And women."

He cocked his head.

"We have a couple of women on the crew. I swear they do ties faster than the rest of us." I winced. "But they face a lot of shit."

"Misogyny?"

"Yep. Some of the men I work with are assholes." I could think of two right off the top of my head. Guys I gave a wide berth to. Guys I wouldn't want to run into in a dark alley at night. They knew I respected the women. I would've defended them—if they'd asked. They'd made it clear, though, they were capable of taking care of themselves.

Didn't mean I didn't watch out.

Didn't mean I wouldn't intervene if necessary.

"As long as you don't feel that way—"

"I don't." I nearly spat out the word.

He appeared completely unperturbed.

I scrunched my nose. "My mom always taught me to respect women. And I listened. Probably helped I wasn't interested in getting into their pants." I shrugged. "I mightn't have been as respectful with guys at first. But that evolved."

"After your mom died."

I both hated and loved how he was coming to know me so well. "Yeah."

"She sounds like a good woman."

"I didn't...I wasn't the man she'd tried to raise me to be."

"But you are now." He tapped the end of my nose in a way I found weirdly endearing.

Special.

"Food needs to be reheated. You like tomatoes?"

I nodded.

He clapped his hands. "Great. I made bacon, tomato, and mayo sandwiches. I can add lettuce if you want."

"Uh, no." I smiled. "I can't remember the last time I had a BLT without the L. A long freaking time."

"Well, then we're good." He rose. "You do what you need to do, and then I'll serve you breakfast in bed." He wore an oversized T-shirt and track pants and looked fucking sexy.

"Uh...are my jeans dry?"

"Nope. Still damp. Guess you'll just have to stay here until they dry." He pointed to the television across from the bed. "We can watch the game in bed." He sauntered out of the room.

And so we did. Well, we tried to. I was a terrible student, because all I wanted was to learn about him. What turned him on. What made him tick. What made him come as hard as a freight train.

I was pretty sure his ass was sore by the time my jeans were dry and I made my way home. I was also pretty certain he was damn happy about it.

Chapter Twelve

Isaiah

"Stop fidgeting." I glared at Travis.

He sighed. "I'm meeting your mother."

We were riding the elevator up to her fifteenth-floor condo. She'd bought a studio condo in this building when I'd moved out. She claimed she didn't mind the small space. In truth, she'd saved her entire life for a place of her own. Tired of renting, she had a dream of home ownership. An unexpected inheritance from a distant maiden aunt had helped a lot. Mom owned the place pretty much outright.

I'd also received a part of that inheritance, and had put it down on my mortgage. I'd renegotiated for a lower payment, so I had a bit more money to spend. Money I'd been trying to spend on Travis.

Which irritated him to no end.

That, in turn, made me grin all the freaking time.

Mom's studio was in an older building in North Vancouver. A quick ride on the ferry got her across the Burrard Inlet and another quick bus down Burrard Street landed her at the hospital. When St. Paul's moved into its new home a few years from now, she'd have to take the SkyTrain. I worried, even though public transit was pretty safe.

I worried about everything to do with her.

The bell chimed, the door opened, and we stepped into the hallway.

"That smells..." Travis sniffed. "Oh my God."

I laughed. "Mom gives some to each of her neighbors. So she was probably walking these hallways about ten minutes ago."

"And we get to eat that?" Travis's stomach actually rumbled.

Another laugh escaped my lips. "Yes, we get to eat that."

"Okay." He took a deep breath. "This, uh, feels fast."

I cocked my head.

"Meeting the parents."

"Mom's been bugging me for weeks. Thanksgiving's the perfect time. She was going to go all-out anyway. This way she doesn't have to do it twice."

"She doesn't *have* to do it at all."

I grasped his hand. "This is my mom's way. She shows love with food." I patted my stomach. "Why do you think I work out so much? Have to keep up with her *love*."

He squeezed my hand. "My mom would've loved you."

"Well, this will be our way of sharing me with her." I wasn't religious, but I was spiritual. On occasion, I believed things beyond what could be explained. I could believe Travis's mom was here in spirit.

"Yeah, okay."

Mom's door swung open. "Good grief, Isaiah. Are you going to stand there and jabber or are you going to come in?"

She eyed Travis. "You're too skinny. I'm going to put some meat on your bones. Now, do you accept hugs or am I being too forward? My son likes to chastise me for stepping into other people's spaces."

"Uh…"

I nudged him forward. I wasn't one hundred percent certain he was ready for a *Mama* hug. But he also hauled steel around for a living.

He was tough.

And then he stepped into my mother's embrace. They were almost the same height and, after a long moment, he sagged against her.

Slowly, I rubbed his back.

He shook under my touch.

Mama soothed, in her gentle way. "Oh, my dear boy. Welcome to my home."

Welcome home was what she meant. Mama's place was home to anyone who needed it. I'd often brought home strays as a kid. We couldn't keep the animals—but some of the kids had become lifelong friends to me and pseudo-adopted children to Mama.

"Okay, ham waits for no one. I hope you like pineapple." Mama finally released Travis, then put her hands on his cheeks.

As I often did.

And she sent the message I always tried to convey.

I see you for who you are. Your beauty on the inside is what I treasure.

Whether he'd be able to accept those sentiments was a challenge. He struggled. He couldn't believe someone like me could care about someone like him. That hurt my heart.

"I love pineapple. And ham." Travis grinned as Mama released him. Then he gave me a glance. Part panic, part relief, part adoration.

Yeah, Mama could engender all those sentiments at the same time.

She bustled back into her condo, wearing her bunny rabbit slippers I'd bought her when she'd moved into the place. I maintained she needed dignified slippers when she greeted guests.

As predicted, she'd laughed uproariously. And had worn them every time I visited since.

Travis and I removed our shoes, then followed her into the condo. She had a pullout couch, a desk, several comfortable chairs, a few bookcases, and a high-top table with four stools. Said table was laden with bowls, containers, and three plates.

"Sit." Mama bustled to the slow cooker.

"Do you need me to carve the ham?" I fingered the electric carving knife.

"Well, yes, that would be lovely."

I always carved the ham.

Mama always acted like she was going to do it herself. She was perfectly capable, but she knew the pleasure I took from this simple action.

"What can I do to help?" Travis stood nervously twisting his hands while standing on the artificial border between the kitchen and the living room. A delineation which was just tile floor to carpeting.

"Sit." Mama motioned to the table. "And maybe turn up the music a bit. I'm playing that all-Christmas music radio station."

I sighed. "I bought you that stereo system. Heck, I even installed it."

She waved at the ham. "Too complicated. I grew up listening to the radio, and so I'll do it now."

Arguing was pointless.

So I carved the honeyed ham while listening to *Silent Night*, *Jingle Bell Rock*, and *Do You See What I See*. Which happened to be my favorite. I cut Travis a glance.

His eyes were a little misty. He clutched his hand to his chest in a way I knew meant he was touched. He'd done the same thing when I'd given him a team jersey. Oh, and tickets to sit beside Becca for our next home game. I'd waffled back and forth between offering just one or giving him the pair. In the end, I'd left it up to him. He'd invited his coworker Annabelle.

The look of gratitude he'd given me would stick with me for a very long time. *I'm going to keep giving him as many gifts as I can. Stuff that doesn't cost money. Stuff that makes him smile.*

Finally, when I had the ham completely carved, Mama moved the plate to the table. She'd send me home with a massive container, and I'd be having ham-and-honey-mustard sandwiches for a week.

I'd be in seventh heaven.

Mama and I sat at the table. I sat next to Travis and took his hand as Mama offered her prayer of thanksgiving. I'd warned him and he'd assured me he didn't mind. That he wouldn't be offended. That he'd respect every tradition in Mama's house.

We hadn't specifically talked religion. Nor had we dug into politics, although he'd mentioned whom he voted for last time. Same party I had, so we were good on that topic. I could've dated someone who didn't see things the way I did—had, in fact. We'd avoided politics, but I'd always had a niggling sense of knowing we perceived things differently. I liked that Travis believed in the same things I did. Understood, with few words, what things were important to me.

"Eat." Mama passed the basket of rolls to Travis.

His nose twitched as he took one.

"Fresh baked." She beamed.

"I..." He cleared his throat. "I don't even know what to say."

"So don't say anything. Eat up, making happy noises, enjoy the meal, and I'll be satisfied. And if you don't like it—"

"Oh, I'm certain I will." He surveyed all the food. "You don't have to worry about that." He put a roll on his plate, then accepted the plate of ham I handed him.

She grunted. "You're too skinny."

"Mama." I tried for my best chastising voice. Evidently I hadn't been clear in my warning not to focus on the physical. I'd warned her about the scar and tattoos. Hadn't thought to mention how skinny he was. And since I knew he didn't do drugs, I wasn't as worried as Mama clearly appeared to be. Drug use by people working in trades was something I'd read about. The numbers scared me.

Travis assured me he was fine.

I believed him.

"So, Travis, you like my son?"

I nearly choked on a piece of ham.

Travis cleared his throat. "Yes, ma'am, I really do."

She waved. "You call me Mama. Everyone calls me Mama. Well, except at work. Then I'm Nurse Maria."

"Uh...Mama..." He appeared to be trying out the word. "Thank you." He whispered the words quietly.

"And..." She held a piece of bun aloft—nearly pointing it at him.

"Yes, Mama, I like your son a lot."

She nodded her approval. "That's good. He likes you too. Talks about you all the time—"

"Mama." I glared.

She grinned. "He doesn't bring boys around."

"I'm hardly a boy." Travis glanced down at his food, pushing a bit of mashed potato around the plate.

I handed him the gravy boat.

He offered me a grateful smile.

"You're younger than me." Mama grinned. "That makes you a boy. To me, anyway."

"That's true."

Although not by much. Mama had me when she was young. She wasn't even fifty to Travis's forty and... "Hey, you're closer in age to my boyfriend than you are to me." I eyed my mother.

She continued to grin. "I wondered how long it would take you to figure that out. I don't care. I just want you to be with a man who makes you happy." She pointed her fork at Travis. "He makes you happy."

I swallowed. "Yeah, he kind of does." I exchanged a glance with Travis.

"Me too."

He offered that shy smile of his that I loved so much. So many little things about him called to me. His smiles—so rare and therefore meaning even more when he offered them. The way he ducked his head—a shyness I found adorable. His keen sense of curiosity—he tried to hide it, but he loved learning new things. He used that knowledge whenever he could. But only with me, as far as I could see. He was afraid of letting people know he was smarter than they perceived him to be.

"So use condoms and be safe." Mama popped the last of her roll in her mouth.

Travis choked on his asparagus.

And we were off.

Chapter Thirteen

Travis

How I survived Thanksgiving dinner at Mama's was quite beyond me. On top of the lecture about safe sex, she'd also given broad hints about not hurting her *baby*, living a clean life, being good to the environment, and taking care of myself.

In vain, I tried to explain that I expended a lot of calories at work, and that was why I was scrawny. I didn't mention my mother'd been wraith-like. Always slender. Not in a bad way—she'd just been willowy.

I took after her.

She never discussed my father, and I'd learned, very early on, never to mention him. As I grew older, and understood child support, I wanted to demand I be allowed to track him down. Even I recognized how hard my mom worked. My father had gotten my mother pregnant—he should've been held responsible.

Only after she died, and I found her journal, did I discover she'd been raped by a stranger.

The few times I'd asked questions now haunted me. But I'd been a child. She'd been right to keep this from me when I was too young to understand. Maybe when I was old enough, she'd figured I didn't need to know. But she'd drilled into me about respecting my partner, the importance of consent, and how I could do real damage if I wasn't careful. I hadn't been great with my partners in those first years after I discovered gay sex—but I'd also never taken what hadn't been freely given.

"Travis?"

"Uh, yeah?" I rubbed my eyes.

"Hon, we're home."

Only now did I realize we were in the parking garage of his condo.

I liked how he called it *home*. He meant his place, but I hadn't had a real home since Mom died. My apartment in the eastside was just a place to hang my hat. "What are we to each other?"

He frowned. "You mean like an actual title?"

"Yeah."

"Well, I told Mama I was bringing home my boyfriend. I don't do that often...well, like at all. I needed her to know how special you are to me. She overplayed her hand, though. Her lectures—" He chuckled. "—yeah, discreet isn't her strong suit."

"I like her. A lot. She cares about you. Wants to protect you. You need to treasure that."

He chuckled. "Oh, I do. You should see her when she comes to my games. She yells as loud as the fans half her age. She's always shouting at the refs if she thinks they made a bad call."

"Like the time you took an elbow to the throat?" He'd told me about that time. The idea terrified me because I'd once seen a brawler nearly kill a guy by doing the same thing.

"She wasn't there that game. But when the guy only got a yellow card, I thought Becca was going to lose her shit. Everyone knew it should've been a red card. Automatically. But I guess the ref had a bad angle. Whatever. I have to say, the other player gave me a wide berth for the rest of the game—which we won handily. Becca could barely speak she was so hoarse."

"You love that woman."

He chuckled. "I really do. Now, what's going on?"

"What are we to each other?"

"Boyfriends isn't enough?" He laughed. Not in a mean way.

"Well, sure. I just...I don't want to make an assumption."

"Badarse?"

"Hmm?"

"You like to boss me around."

I didn't do it as often as I liked—given we were new to this relationship—but the answer came easily. "Yeah, I do."

"And I like being bossed around." Despite his tanned skin, a pronounced blush crossed his cheeks.

"Well, that's true."

"I care about you."

"And I care about you."

"So let's do boyfriends. It's too soon for me to ask you to move in, although if you brought more clothes over, I wouldn't complain."

My jaw dropped. "It's been three weeks."

He shrugged. "I know what I want. I want you. You don't appear to have any objections—"

"I don't."

"—then it's super simple. We're together. As a couple. You come to my games. I worry about you while you're at work. Seems pretty simple to me."

I swallowed. "It does, doesn't it?"

He grasped my hand. "Life doesn't have to be complicated. I get that it has been for you. That you've had a tough life. If I can make it easier, then I want to do that."

"You already have."

He raised an eyebrow.

I smoothed it with my callused finger. "By being you."

He leaned toward me.

I unbuckled my seatbelt and met him halfway.

The kiss was simple, sweet, and tender.

"You taste like coffee." Mama had served a rich Turkish coffee for dessert. I'd expected something more traditional, but she'd agreed to take a shift at the hospital because someone was sick. She'd needed the caffeination.

I wasn't certain Mallow and I did, but of course we'd gone along with what Mama wanted. We'd offered to drive her to the hospital, but she'd claimed she wanted the walk down to the SeaBus to refresh her. Personally, I figured we could've dropped her a block or two from the hospital, but I'd quickly discovered Mama moved to the beat of her own drum.

"I like coffee." Mallow pulled back. "But now I'm wired. At least we don't have to work or have practice tomorrow."

Some families celebrated Thanksgiving on the actual statutory holiday—the Monday. Mama preferred the Sunday night—if she had the time off.

Mallow pressed a hand to his stomach. "I think I need to burn off some of those calories."

"Me too."

He winked. "Mama won't be happy. She wants to fatten you up."

"I'm just naturally slender."

"I know. It's teasing. With Mama love thrown in."

"Well, if she wants to feed me like that all the time, I have no objections." I winced. "That sounded bad."

"Huh?"

"Like that I expect your mother to cook for me. I should, you know, reciprocate. Invite her to my place. Just..." I winced again.

He tapped my nose. "Mama would welcome an invitation. You said it was small. But clean."

"I'd hire a cleaner to make it Mama clean. But it's dark." I was on the north side of a building that buttressed up against another building. I never saw sunlight. Hell, I barely saw daylight. At night, though, with my blackout blinds, my bedroom was pitch-black dark.

"Travis?"

His use of my proper name caught my attention. He didn't do that often. Just like I almost never called him Isaiah. He said he preferred Mallow. And I believed him. "Yes?"

"I want to go upstairs and make love. Nice and soft and gentle."

"That sounds nice."

"Exactly. We'll let the food settle while we fool around. Then we'll make love. Then I'll sleep all night in your arms."

Despite me being the smaller guy, I was almost always the big spoon. I wanted to feel like I was protecting *my man*. No one had ever stayed. No one had ever let me be the protector. The guys hadn't minded me being the Dominant. But they hadn't wanted more than rough sex and bossiness.

Mallow wanted it all.

"Yes, let's go upstairs. We have another day." And I liked the idea of bringing my things over. His place was so close to my work that I could walk. Well, short hike. That meant I didn't have to pay for parking for the bike. Or worry about it getting stolen.

Mallow had gotten permission from his condo board to allow me to park it in his parking space with his car. Made for a tight fit, but I didn't have to worry about overstaying my welcome in the visitor spots.

We made our way to the elevators. I pressed myself against Mallow's body as he pressed the button for his floor.

On the ground floor, though, the door opened.

An older couple, with a little dog, took us in before proceeding to join us.

I tried to move away.

Mallow gripped me closer. "Good evening Mathilda. Ronald." He grinned "Hello, Petey."

The little dog lunged at him.

I held my breath.

"Petey." The man, Ronald, tried to pull the dog back.

Mallow gently untangled himself from me. He crouched, holding out his hand for Petey to sniff. "You're still a puppy. But you need to listen to your daddy."

Inwardly, I groaned.

"We're in obedience training." Mathilda rolled her eyes. "You can see how well that's going. We forgot to put on his harness for the walk, and he's nearly choked himself several times."

Mallow gently petted the dog. "Puppy energy. You let me know if you ever need a break. My boyfriend and I would be happy to take Petey for a long walk. Tire him out."

"That's mighty kind of you." Ronald nodded to me. "We might just take you up on that."

The bell chimed for our floor.

Clearly reluctantly, Mallow rose. "You have my number." He put his arm around my back and guided me out of the elevator.

I was, of course, perfectly capable of doing it myself. But I liked the protective nature of his gesture. Marking his territory. Completely unnecessary with this older couple, but making a statement nonetheless.

They waved to us as the door closed.

I exhaled.

"They're good people." Mallow pressed a kiss to my cheek.

"Sure. But I worry about what people will think."

"They'll think they no longer have to try to set me up." He said that with a huge grin.

Apparently Johnnie and Roger were continuously trying to set Mallow up with guys. Twinks and bottoms. They were truly clueless about Mallow's preferences, and he hadn't known how to convey his preferences to his friends. My appearance clarified things. Hence the comment, that first night, about me not being what they expected. I'd taken that the wrong way, naturally. They'd just meant I wasn't a twink. Whether Mallow had explained the whole top and bottom thing? I hadn't asked. "Take me to bed?"

"With pleasure."

Mamba hung out in the living room alone.

We made gentle love that night.

Well, the first time.

The second time I fucked him into the mattress and made him scream.

Thank God for good soundproofing.

Chapter Thirteen

Travis

I felt the crunch of bone from the stands.

Well, no bone had actually broken.

Or at least I hoped not.

"Oh God, oh God, oh God." Carsyn squealed.

Carsyn? Carly? Corey?

Damn, I couldn't remember.

Johnnie had gone on three dates with her, and somehow she'd wrangled tickets out of him.

Becca had used a very unflattering name for the woman when she'd arrived.

I could admit her pink sequined crop top, white jeans, and jean jacket, along with her sandal high heels didn't exactly fit the near-freezing temperature of the Sunday afternoon game. At least the rain had stopped.

"Johnnie! Yoo-hoo? Are you okay, babydoll?"

Becca, who thank God was on my right side—and therefore likely out of hearing range of the squealing woman on my other—snickered.

As far as I could tell, and again to my relief, Johnnie couldn't hear Carsyn above the shouts of the crowd at the refs for only using a yellow card and not the red ejection card they all felt was warranted.

In my ignorance, I sat back and let people howl their displeasure.

Mallow had spent many, many, many hours teaching me the intricacies of the game. At first, he rewarded me for getting things right.

Soon he started rewarding effort when I got it wrong.

Eventually he gave up trying to teach me, and we spent all our spare time in bed.

Most days, when not practicing, he taught physical education at a local school. He'd neglected to mention he'd somehow obtained a bachelor's degree and a teaching certificate. All by the age of twenty-five.

Plus a professional rugby player. Which didn't pay nearly as much as it should have, given the physical punishment of the game.

Carsyn gripped my arm.

No, Carly. Right. Carly.

"Is he going to be okay?"

"Well, he's walking off the field, so I suspect so." Johnnie wasn't even limping, so I took solace in that.

"He'll be fine." Becca spoke loud enough for everyone in three rows to hear. "He's a tough bastard."

"Mom." Cassandra appeared mortified, given her red cheeks.

I chuckled to myself because, not twenty seconds earlier, she'd been one of the spectators howling about the *bad call* and the *crappy refereeing*.

The girl amused me to no end. And since tomorrow was her twelfth birthday, Isaiah and I had a gift for her.

My man knew the birthdate of every child of every teammate. Written down on a huge calendar, thank God.

Francine, the trainer, continued to work on Johnnie's knee.

"He might be out for the rest of the game." Becca blew out a breath. "He's the best hooker. They *need* him."

I didn't laugh. Came close...but managed not to.

Suddenly, there was a loose ball.

Okay, scrum time.

This part amused me to no end. A bunch of guys huddling and pushing against each other while another guy tried to get the ball, and—

Bam, they were off.

The sideways tossing continued until Roger crossed the line.

Cheers, hoots, and hollers went up from the crowd.

Roger held the ball aloft in triumph while Cassandra whistled. Then she shouted. "Way to go, Dad."

Louder than anything her mother had done so far this game.

Finally, the match ended. Vancouver won by ten. And Johnnie hadn't returned to the game.

To my relief, and shame for the relief, he grabbed Carly, and they headed out. If they were going to get drinks, good for them. If they were going to have sex? Yeah, whatever.

Becca and Cassandra went home, so I was invited to join the crew at the local brew pub.

I noticed I was the only guy. "What about the wives and girl-friends?" I nudged Isaiah.

"Not tonight."

"Yet, I'm here."

He cocked his head.

"Well, am I not one of the girlfriends?" I used air quotes.

He considered. "Some of them went to the bar down the road to share cosmos. Did you want to join them?"

"They all drink cosmos?"

"No, some enjoy beer. You get what I'm saying." He sighed. "You think we're being sexist."

I shook my head. "I just figured you'd all want to celebrate with the game."

"Tonight's special."

"Huh?"

"Jason's getting married next month."

In early December. I remembered. A rugby-themed wedding because Sonya was as nuts about the game as he was. And she was also tolerant of the salty-mouthed parrot, Wally.

"So this is the bachelor party—only he doesn't know it. Just like Sonya's at the bachelorette party. A bunch of her girlfriends are joining, and—" He was cut off by the arrival of two massively huge guys.

Jason rose. "What are you doing here?"

"You think I was going to miss my baby brother's bachelor party?" The bigger of the brutes pulled Jason into a hug.

Jason was a big guy. His brother easily had an extra three inches and thirty pounds on him.

"Surprise!" The entire table broke into cheers and cries.

Fortunately, none of the other patrons appeared perturbed by our raucousness. Likely why they chose this bar. *And Johnnie's missing this.* That caused a pang because he really loved spending time with his crew.

Jason's brother and best friend from high school pulled up chairs, and the festivities began.

I had one beer—as did Isaiah.

He was driving us home tonight.

I'd made noises about getting a bigger bike so we could ride together.

He called it a death machine and asked me to consider getting an SUV. He said he'd even pay for the extra parking spot in his building.

That kind of warmed my heart. In all these years, no one cared that I rode a motorcycle. Well, Dodge teased me about being an organ donor. At first I hadn't understood because, of course, I had a card saying I would be one. He'd meant that riders of motorcycles tended to die more frequently, on a per capita basis, and so we were more likely to be organ donors. He'd laughed.

I'd had to think some more about that.

Jason thoroughly enjoyed himself. No doubt in my mind as he laughed, put up with the ribbing, demanded to know where the strippers were, then pretended mock offense when none showed up.

Isaiah assured me that had never been in the cards. Frankly, too much respect for women to objectify them.

That'd surprised and pleased me. I had enough of that shit at work. If I heard one more story about a *titty club*, I was going to lose my shit. Always said in front of Annabelle, of course. Sometimes I wondered if she might be bi or lesbian or something, but I never asked. Never would. Her business and hers alone.

The car ride home from the pub was quick, and soon we were brushing our teeth and heading to bed.

Isaiah raised an eyebrow as I crawled into bed.

Naked, of course.

"What?"

"Does this feel...domestic...to you?"

I stilled. "Is that a bad thing? You asked me to stay over tonight."

"Because it's closer to your work. I always want you to stay over. I'd be happier if you just never left."

I blinked. "Like move in with you?"

"Well, yeah." All casual.

He slid into bed next to me. Naked, of course.

"This is a small place. You're going to get tired of me and all my shit."

"Your furniture might be a tight fit."

"My furniture isn't worth a storage fee. I can give it away and would be lucky if someone took it."

"There are places to donate to. People in transitional housing. New immigrants. Students. Your stuff is sturdy."

He'd been to my place all of once—but had obviously been observant.

"There's enough space here for your stuff. We can make it work. Or I can look at buying a two-bedroom condo in the building. They come up for sale periodically."

He wouldn't be able to afford the mortgage on a two-bedroom.

Not without help.

"Are you suggesting we buy a place together?" I had some money set aside. Money for my retirement since my work didn't offer a pension plan. Since one bad injury could sideline me forever. But I could invest that in a down payment. "You're serious."

"Yeah, Travis. I really am."

"We've known each other just over a month."

"Do you want to see other people?"

"Hell fucking no. And I don't want you to either." I winced. "But that's not up to me."

"We're boyfriends. In a monogamous relationship. It's very much up to you." He pulled me against him so my chin rested on his chest as I gazed at him.

"You're sure."

"As much as I can be about anything."

"Then yeah, let's do this." My stomach went into freefall, but I also felt a certainty I hadn't...perhaps ever in my life.

The next week I gave away my furniture and moved into Isaiah's place.

I did not, however, give up my bike.

Compromises.

Chapter Fourteen

Isaiah

"This is a bad idea." Travis gripped his armrests. "A really bad idea."

"Are you sure you don't want the window seat?" I sipped my water as if this was an everyday occurrence. Because, for me, it was.

"No, I don't want the window seat. First, you'll be uncomfortable and worried about cramming the poor lady on the aisle."

The lady who had put in her earbuds and was clearly ignoring both of us.

"Secondly, when we crash, I don't want a front-row seat."

"We're not in the front row." I took another sip. "I care for you deeply, but even I couldn't spring for two business-class tickets."

"You shouldn't have sprung for these." He glanced around.

Somehow, the moment he agreed to my harebrained scheme, the tickets had magically appeared. Like they'd been sitting in the cart for the airline, waiting for me to hit *buy*. He'd had to get an expedited passport and voilà. Here we were.

"I wasn't going to let you back out. The tickets are nonrefundable." I sniffed. "You wouldn't want to waste the money."

"I still think Mama could've asked for the time off work. Doesn't she have seniority or something?"

"Her friend Myles is a new father. She wanted him to have time with the baby and his wife. You can't fault Mama for having a soft spot for babies. And she's also taking care of Mamba." I'd repeated these points several times, but Travis never quite looked convinced. And somehow I'd talked him into requesting two weeks off work.

Apparently, his supervisor had been so surprised, she'd just stamped the request and shooed him out of her office. In twenty years, he'd always taken a payout in lieu of vacation.

Once I'd seen the amount he'd given me for the down-payment, I could see how missing all those vacations had paid off. He was just a spendthrift and hadn't wanted me to know about his nest egg when we'd first started dating. I respected that.

"We're going to crash."

"We are not going to crash. Thousands of planes take off and land safely without crashing."

"But planes *do* crash."

I arched an eyebrow. "Construction workers get injured more often. You don't see me asking you to quit your job." I wanted to. But I never would. He lived his life. I lived mine.

Just like when he'd watched me have my face slammed into the ground during the last game. He'd wanted to beg me to find something...less physically violent.

He hadn't, though. At least he hadn't come right out and done it. So I'd held my tongue about the skyscraper.

The flight attendant began his explanation of the rules.

Badarse gripped the pamphlet and followed along carefully. He'd reluctantly admitted having taken some extra English classes after finishing his high school equivalency because he hadn't wanted to appear illiterate. Those classes had helped when he'd taken the construction-management courses at the British Columbia Institute of Technology.

All of which he'd said with trepidation. As if I'd judge him. Either as being too smart for his job or stupid—his word—for needing the extra schooling.

Right, like I, of all people, would judge someone strong enough to ask for help when they needed it.

I was so fucking proud of him.

And had heard the airline attendant's spiel at least once a month for years now. Dutifully, though, I paid attention.

In case Travis had any questions.

He said he preferred *Badarse* most of the time.

A way to keep that barrier between the two of us. And between him and the rest of the world.

When we were with Mama or his friend Dodge, though, he was just Travis. When we were alone, he was *my Travis*.

Hence coaxing him into taking a fourteen-hour flight from Vancouver to Auckland, and another quick hop to Christchurch. A trip I did at least twice a year.

He let out a long breath. "You're sure this is safe?"

"Cross my heart."

He arched an eyebrow. "The rest of that saying is *hope to die*."

"Uh...huh."

"Yeah. Nothing to say about that, eh?"

"Nope. Silence is the better part of virtue. Or some shit like that."

We finished taxiing, and the engines roared.

Travis gripped my hand.

Next thing I knew, we were hurtling down the runway.

I loved this. The aerodynamics involved in flight. The complexity of the machine we were in. That we were essentially a tin can flying through the air at incomprehensible speeds.

Being in the air was my happy place.

Fourteen hours later, I could admit it hadn't been poor Travis's.

We'd encountered a lot of turbulence.

He'd been violently ill. To the point the nice lady on the aisle traded her seat for mine, I took the middle seat, and Travis sat on the end. Fortunately we were close to the bathroom. A couple of times, he needed the airsickness bags.

I'd felt incredibly guilty and, as we waited for our flight to Christchurch, I seriously contemplated renting a car and driving us the sixteen hours. But that wouldn't be any better, and I wanted Nana's whitebait so badly, my saliva glands were working overtime.

We'd won our last three games. Although my shoulder was sore from a knee to it—hello, ouch—I was doing okay. Even survived the cramped quarters of the flight.

Which gave me an idea.

I headed over to the gate agent and gave her my most winsome smile. "Uh, I don't suppose you have room in first class, do you?"

She checked her screen. "Two. Last-minute cancellation. We're about to see if someone wants to pay to upgrade."

I pulled out my credit card. "My boyfriend was sick all the way from Canada. His first flight. He doesn't even want to get on the plane."

She gently pushed the credit card back. "Well, for the good of the other passengers, he should be seated as close to the washroom as I can get him." She snagged my boarding pass. "I hope someday someone does this for my brother and his boyfriend."

"How old?"

"Seventeen and completely smitten. They play rugby together."

"Oh, I play."

She eyed me. "Professionally?"

"Yes. In Vancouver."

"The Orcas?"

I blinked.

She grinned. "Grew up in a rugby household. If there's a team whose name I don't know, it's because I've forgotten."

"Would you..." I gestured to her Sharpie.

She grinned.

I opened my bag and brought out one of my photos. I loathed the things, but Nana insisted I bring one home for each of her grandchildren. I kept a couple in my bag and the rest were crammed into my suitcase.

The gate agent handed me the marker, and I signed her photo with a flourish.

She handed me the new boarding passes.

I made my way back over to Travis. "I have a treat for you."

"Ginger candy?"

"And some anti-nausea meds. Which you should take now. No, a special treat."

"You charmed someone." He eyed me, with one bloodshot dull-blue eye. "You're up to something. I saw you."

"Just act casual when we get the best seats on the plane."

"Sure, I can do that." He pressed a hand to his forehead.

"You going to be okay?"

"Just make certain we've got every airsick bag on the flight. And maybe extras."

I did ensure we had a few extras but, in the end, we didn't need them. The flight was brilliantly perfect, and we landed without so much as a belly clench from my boyfriend.

Fortunately, my uncle Peter picked us up and spirited us away to his spare bedroom. He kept the family at bay while Travis and I slept for about twenty hours. Finally, we awoke feeling almost normal. A simple breakfast of eggs and fruit settled our stomachs, and we were soon ready to greet the family.

Well, I was.

Travis was fucking terrified.

"If you can survive your first flight, you can take on my family."

"I'm taking a cruise ship back to Canada."

"You'll get seasick."

He pressed a hand to his belly. "I'll swim. I'm never doing this shit again. Ever."

"Uncle Izzy! Uncle Izzy!"

Six of the younger nieces and nephews barreled into the room.

I offered Travis a sheepish shrug.

He sat up straighter.

And we were off.

Chapter Fifteen

Travis

Mallow's family was...something else. Like, the first night, to celebrate his homecoming, they threw a barbecue in his honor. I lost track at about fifty people, but apparently two hundred and two showed up.

Nana was in her element. She directed her many minions to do all the cooking, food organizing, and beach activities as the sun set over the ocean.

I didn't remember ever seeing such stunning colors. But then, when had I ever paid attention to the sky? Occasionally, Dodge would nudge me and I'd look up from my work to see a beautiful sunrise or sunset. Most of the time, though, I kept my head down and did my work. The more ties, the better.

Now, though, with the pink, purple, yellow, and scarlet skies—along with beautiful puffy clouds—I could acknowledge what I'd missed in my life.

Tiki torches were lit and Nana insisted I sit next to her as a group of the men did some funky dance. Then the women did some neat stuff as well.

Isaiah tried to explain the significance of everything.

I did my best to understand, but the magic of the moment carried me away.

Nana tapped my arm as another dance ended. "Have you had enough to eat?"

I patted my stomach. "Completely full."

She tisked. "Need more food."

I'd already put on about five pounds since meeting Mallow and Maria. And yes, she'd have fattened me up even more if she could.

Every night she wasn't working, she invited us over.

Mallow would gently extend our regrets about half the time, knowing she was run off her feet at work and not wanting her to fuss over the two of us.

Still, as each visit passed, I felt more and more like I had a second mother. My mother'd been estranged from her parents—after she got pregnant with me and hadn't told them—so I'd never known my grandparents.

Now, with Nana by my side, I longed for what could have been.

And celebrated what was.

"I'm okay with the amount I've eaten."

Her nose twitched. "Stomach still upset from the plane? Tomorrow we'll get some more fruit into you. To calm your stomach."

I didn't remember fruit as a remedy for an upset stomach, but I sure as shit wasn't going to question Nana's wisdom.

She leaned over. "Isaiah is so very much like his father."

I stilled.

"A better man, though." She sighed. "I loved my son, but he wasn't the most responsible of men. I understood why Maria didn't want to come back to live with us after he left."

Maria had been visiting New Zealand when she'd been wooed by Mallow's dad. They'd married and had Mallow. She'd stayed in Christchurch until her husband had taken off with another man. She'd filed for divorce, packed up Mallow, and headed back to Canada. Mallow was a dual citizen.

"I think..." I cleared my throat. "She once said she'd loved him."

"Smitten." Nana smiled. The fire sparked light in her dark-brown eyes. Eyes so like Mallow's. "They shouldn't have married. Too young. Too impetuous. But neither could be talked out of it. When she left, my heart broke. I might have twenty-one grandchildren, but Isaiah always had a special place in my heart."

Which blew my mind. Not the special part—that was a given. Especially with his gentle personality. No, the fact Nana had six children, twenty-one grandchildren, and nine great-grandchildren. So far, as she liked to say. She'd confided she wanted Isaiah to have children, then casually asked if I wanted them as well.

I nearly choked on papaya juice. I'd sputtered. Settling had taken a while because, as I watched Mallow surrounded by all the kids, I could totally see him as a father.

As I thought about my solitary life, I couldn't envision a family.

Probably should've had that conversation before *you moved in, eh?*

Yeah, yeah. No *probably* about it. If we'd been a hetero couple, that would've been top on the agenda. Being gay didn't really absolve us of the tough stuff. I'd just been so damn eager to share my life with him. I'd never considered my life might involve so many...children.

Becca was already dropping broad hints about us babysitting so she and Roger could get some alone time before the next child arrived.

Their youngest was still in diapers—which terrified me. I had to google how to put a diaper on a toddler.

Fascinating.

And something I never saw myself doing. Nope, that would be Mallow's job. And I'd rope Cassandra into helping me keep the little ones occupied.

See? I had everything worked out.

Except...my heart.

"I'm going to bed." Nana squeezed my arm.

"Do you need an escort home?" Somehow, the three houses on either side of Nana's were owned by various members of her family. Tonight's party was at Peter's and he lived one door down from his mother.

I wasn't certain how I'd feel about Maria living in the condo next to ours. But I'd welcome her—especially if Mallow was happy. Anything to make Mallow happy.

"Paul will escort me." She snapped her fingers, and a nephew approached.

"Hi, Nana."

"I'm ready."

"Of course." He offered his arm. He was...

I scratched my chin. Nope, I couldn't remember whose child he was. I needed Mallow to make a whiteboard with all the family. Well, maybe not all two hundred and two.

Nana eyed me for a long moment. "You'll do." Then she and Paul were gone.

Everyone waved and a few family members hugged her, but soon enough she'd disappeared.

Mallow dropped into her vacant chair.

"Isn't that sacrilege?"

"Shh." He grinned. "I won't say anything if you won't."

"Isn't that my line?"

"Nana loves me."

"That she does."

"She wants me to move home."

"You *are* half Kiwi." The thought of losing him, so soon after I'd found him, nearly broke me.

He shifted uncomfortably. "I got a call today."

I blinked. "When?"

"You were passed out on the bed. I happened to be awake, so I snuck out of the room to check it."

This is bad. He didn't want to tell me and...it's bad. "And? Don't keep me in suspense." I tried to laugh at that.

It sounded forced.

Apparently to both of us because he winced.

"The coach of the All Blacks wants to meet me."

"The..." I scrunched my nose. "That's the New Zealand rugby team."

"Yeah."

"The best team in the world."

"Uh..." He pursed his lips. "The New Zealand Women won the 7s."

"And Canada took silver." I sat a little straighter. See? I was paying attention.

"Women and men are currently third. But like we're less than two points out of the top spot."

"And Canada?" Apparently I hadn't been paying enough attention.

"Women are second and men's..." He sighed.

"Ah. So playing for New Zealand?"

"The All Blacks? Dream come true."

"When's the meeting?"

"Two days after Christmas."

"Where?" My gut churned.

"He happens to be in Christchurch."

"Well, do you want me to drive you?" A big joke because people here drove on the wrong side of the road and, although I was pretty adept at things, shifting with my left arm intimidated me. There, I admitted it—I wasn't keen to drive. Pretty much a first.

"He's not going to ask me to join the squad."

"But he might ask you to try out."

"I'm Canadian."

"You're half Kiwi."

"He probably just wants intel on the Canadian team."

"Which you won't give him." I might not know *everything* about my boyfriend—but I knew that much.

He snagged my hand. "He's not going to ask me."

"You don't *know* that. You're one of Canada's best fullbacks."

"Who has to work a second job to pay the mortgage. I'm not even a full-time player."

I scowled. I hadn't realized how little some athletes were paid. I'd heard the salaries for professional hockey, baseball, basketball, and football players and had assumed other athletes were at least making enough to live off.

Spending time with Mallow had taught me how far off those assumptions were. "Are we arguing?"

He leaned over to press a kiss to my cheek. "It would be, like, our first time. So let it not be about something we can't change."

Could we really not change it? "If they ask you to try out, you need to. If you make the squad, you have to move here and play for them.

Even if you're on the bench a lot at the beginning, I think you need to do this."

He held my gaze. "Do you want me to move?"

My scowl deepened. *God, is he really this dense?* Not even factoring that I wouldn't have a home if he moved here, I didn't want to lose him. I'd only just *found* him. "I want you to be happy. If that means playing with one of the best teams in the world, then I'm supportive."

"And if that means languishing with a lesser-known team?"

"You're not exactly languishing. You play almost every game. You're integral to the team. You're—"

"Going to take the meeting because one doesn't turn down a meeting like that, but I am also not interested. You're right. I'll be a bench-warmer at best. That's if I even move up onto the squad."

I didn't say you'd be a benchwarmer. You'd be the best fullback on the entire fucking team. Except I didn't know the depth of the bench. He'd talked about the All Blacks before. Had even said there was a series about them. We'd planned to watch it when we went back to Canada.

"He did procure two tickets for a game before we go home. In Wellington. That means more flying."

The urge to hurl overwhelmed, but I fought it down. "Whenever, wherever. I'm there, okay?" Because what was a little barf between lovers?

His eyes glittered—much as his grandmother's had. "Yeah, sounds good."

Chapter Sixteen

Isaiah

Nana eyed me.

I stared right back. I wouldn't be intimidated by a seventy-nine-year-old woman.

Even if my fifty-year-old mother scared the shit out of me.

Somewhere between *respecting my elders* and *standing on my own two feet* lay the answer to this dilemma.

I broke first. "He didn't offer me a spot on the squad. He offered me the opportunity to try out for one of the regional teams."

She arched an eyebrow. "You could come home."

"Nana." I grasped her hand. "New Zealand hasn't been my *home* in twenty years. And, as much as I love everyone here, I'm not leaving Mama."

She pursed her lips. She wasn't my mother's biggest fan. Something about fleeing the country with me after my father left.

Mama was more gracious and deferential to Nana when we visited together.

But the key was *visited*. Because we always went home to Canada.

Nana sniffed. "Well, at least you come to visit. And bring your man."

One of my nieces giggled as she stood by Travis. He was surrounded by teenagers.

He turned to Henry. "Sure, I can look at your bike later. I'm not a mechanic, but I'm pretty good at tune-ups. We'll see. But don't ride it until we know it's safe. You don't want an accident."

Henry dutifully nodded.

Travis put his hands on his hips. He turned to my niece, Patti. "No way are you going back to him. If your man forgets your birthday after you've been together three years, then you need to dump him."

Great. I hadn't even realized she had been in a relationship that long.

Then he turned to Jude. "Of course you have to say you're sorry if you looked at a girl while you were out with your girlfriend. What kind of bull—" He winced. "Bull crap is that? You respect the woman you're with. If you can't—whether because you're not in love with her or just because you're an ass—" Another wince. "Then you let her down gently and get your, uh, stuff together before you start dating someone else. You have to respect the woman you're with."

He gazed at a younger niece. "And you don't go chasing guys twice your age. He's twenty-eight. You're fifteen. That's a hard no."

"You're sixteen years older than Uncle Izzy."

He chuckled. "He's way over the legal age, and I didn't say the relationship wasn't ill-advised."

I nearly rose at that, but Nana gripped my hand, encouraging me to stay where I was. Clearly Travis didn't realize we could hear him.

"But I love your uncle. And I think he loves me. We have respect for each other. If his guy really loves you, then he'll wait until you're at least eighteen. Even better, twenty-two and with a university degree."

"I suppose." Marisol pouted.

Travis gently tapped her chin. "If it's meant to be, waiting won't be a big deal. But you might meet someone your age."

"Are you going to marry Uncle Izzy?" Patti. Never known for discretion.

Badarse drew in a deep breath. "That's a huge commitment. We've only known each other a couple of months."

"Uncle Peter says you're living together." The tenacious girl jutted her chin in defiance.

Travis winced. "Well, yeah. Moving in together made sense."

"But you're not married." Marisol wagged her finger. "Nana says we have to marry before we live with someone."

"But Paul isn't." Patti leaned in. "He's living *in sin* with his boyfriend."

Paul's cheeks reddened.

"How old is Paul?" Travis met her gaze.

"Twenty-six."

"And his boyfriend?"

"Twenty-seven." Again, she tried to jut her chin.

"So something completely different. And, in time, Paul might decide to get married. Living in sin isn't the worst thing in the world, but there's something to be said for marriage."

"Fifty percent of marriages end in divorce." Marisol scrunched her nose.

"Not in this family." Nana spoke loudly to be heard over the surf. Her words had the group turning, thereby giving away our little spot behind the foliage of a bush.

Travis's cheeks turned a Rudolph-nose red.

I grinned.

Nana pushed off her chair and headed toward the group. "Only one of my children has gotten divorced. Only two grandchildren. We choose our mates carefully. We marry for life."

"Izzy's parents divorced." Patti again.

Nana poked her finger at her grandchild. "I didn't say it never happens. I'm saying we encourage family to pick their partners carefully. Isaiah might not realize it yet, but he's picked a splendid mate in Travis. But they're taking their time. No sense rushing. And yes, they're living together in sin. As Travis pointed out, they're old enough to know better and do it anyway." She linked her arm with Travis's. "Now, young man, I want you to walk down the beach with me."

Travis shot me a panicked gaze over her head.

I shrugged with a huge smile.

They headed down the beach.

I leaned back, closing my eyes and enjoying the sun. Summers could get warm and, although I visited often, I still couldn't reconcile the heat with Christmas. I was a good Canadian boy who loved his snow—even if Vancouver almost never saw a white Christmas.

My reverie was interrupted by a small body landing on my lap.

"Unca Izzy, read." Pippa dropped a picture book in my hands. She was all of five and one of the bravest of all the kids—which was saying something.

I worried she'd be a holy terror when she got older. But then, truly, she'd fit in with this crew.

I smiled. "Yes, pumpkin, whatever you'd like."

Chapter Seventeen

Travis

"So you have a month to find a new house back in Canada."

I nearly tripped over the sand—which would've been, like, really pathetic. Except I'd never been in sand. Or if I had, it'd been a million years ago. I was a child of the city. The concrete jungle. All my playgrounds had been asphalt. God help you if you fell. Skinned knees, anyone? "What the fu...dge are you talkin' about? Isaiah has a nice condo. Houses are expensive in Vancouver."

Nana halted.

I did as well. And faced her.

"No. You make Isaiah sell his condo and buy a big house. My cousin's daughter, Alicia, is coming to Canada soon. I expect her to stay with you, and you look after her while she's there at university."

I blinked. "Uh. No way. I mean, what the fu.. dge?"

"Nope—you must do as I say."

I just stared.

"Yes. And Libby's boy, Patrick, will be needing somewhere to stay in a couple of months. He can stay with you."

"With us?" I sort of felt like a broken record. Because even though the words changed, the disbelief didn't.

She tapped her chin. "Yes. Matthew is getting into trouble at school—maybe we'll send him to you for six months and get him away from the bad influence." She grinned. "And there you go. You're going to make all our problems go away."

"Me and Mallow?"

She cocked her head.

"Sorry, me and Isaiah? Isaiah and I?" Man, grammar should've been the last thing on my mind.

"Yes. It is decided. You go home and buy a house."

I started doing the calculations in my mind. Maybe if we bought something in the suburbs. We could pool his money from the condo and the money I'd saved for my retirement. I could work another few years. Or maybe forever.

Whatever. *If* Mallow wanted this, then we'd find a way to make it work.

"You're a smart man." She pressed a hand against my heart. "You'll figure it out."

"Uh...sure..." I was in no way convinced, but I'd damn well do my best.

Later that night, as we sat around the bonfire, Mallow tugged me close. We hadn't spoken all day. Nana had me doing various tasks, chores, and—of all things—helping out in the kitchen.

Libby had been kind, considerate, and—above all else—patient.

I was a slow learner, but I didn't fuck up anything too badly, so dinner had been served on time.

"What did Nana say?" Mallow whispered the words into my ear as the children danced around in an attempt to replicate their parents' performance from a couple of nights previous.

To varying degrees of success.

"I'm not sure you want to know."

He nuzzled behind my ear.

My favorite spot. Which meant I was putty in his hands.

"She says I need to convince you to sell your condo and buy a house so all your family can come and stay. Hell, she wants some to move in."

"Mmm." He nipped my earlobe. "What did you say?"

"What the fuck?" I swallowed. "Okay, maybe *what the fudge*?"

He laughed.

"I'm trying to be serious, Isaiah."

He pulled back. Whether because of my tone or because of my using his proper name, I wasn't certain. He touched my cheek. "What are you afraid of?"

"I'm not—" I stopped abruptly. Of course I was terrified. Who wouldn't be? We'd known each other three months. I'd never had any stable relationship in my life. My mother had been gone longer than I'd had her. I never did more than one-night stands. Hell, my right hand got more use than me being with other people. So the idea of spending the rest of my life with someone—anyone—terrified me.

But I was especially petrified because this was Mallow. *My* Mallow. The man I loved. I'd told the kids as much this morning and, after Nana made her appearance, I realized she, and Mallow, had probably overheard us. "I'm afraid of disappointing you." I pointed to my face. "A face only a mother could love." Something I'd repeated to myself over and over. Only my mother had never had that opportunity. And I certainly hadn't sought out anyone who might disagree.

Mallow cocked his head. "Have you looked around lately?"

I did a quick sweep of the group. "Uh, sure...?"

"And did you notice Paul's tattoos? And Peter's? And Libby's?"

"Well, yeah."

He snorted. "Sweetheart, I'm surrounded by ink. I've chosen not to get tattoos while I'm playing, but I'll certainly get them once I retire. Where they can be covered up so I don't have a problem with the school board. When I retire from teaching, though, I'll do my forearms, hands, and face. This is part of who I am. I might be a good Canadian boy, but my heart is also here. With my family. I want to express that as well. In good time."

"So you don't...?" I waved in the direction of my face.

"Think you're some kind of criminal? Or that someone slashed your face in a knife fight?" He snickered. "I know you're not a bad guy—in any sense of the word—and an industrial accident by a careless employer doesn't reflect on you. It reflects poorly on them, and they should've faced steeper punishments. But none of that matters. Literally. All I see is the man I love." He grinned. "The man who, I believe, told my nieces and nephews this morning that he loved me."

"Uh...you overheard that?"

"What? You giving great advice? Yes. Because obviously you care. And that means everything to me. So they're coming to stay, eh? I guess we'll have to find a way to get a house."

I squinted into the fire. "I might've snuck a look at Vancouver real estate."

He laughed. "Oh dear."

"I might've found a place in the east end. Near where I used to live. On a nice street, though. It's a down-to-the-studs gut job. Will take a lot of money both to buy and to renovate."

"Well, that's not a problem."

"Oh really? How's that?"

"Three things." He gave me *that* look.

"Okay...hit me."

"First, I have some equity in my condo."

"And I have my retirement savings." He had to know I was invested in this—however we were going to make it work.

"We might not need that."

I started to speak.

He placed a finger to my lips.

I desisted.

"Second, there's an inheritance. Each grandchild gets a small amount either when they marry or when they turn thirty."

"I'm amazed everyone isn't married."

"Ah, but Nana has to approve. And before you ask, she's given us her blessing. If we marry, that small inheritance is mine."

"I don't want her to think I'm marrying you for the money."

He guffawed. "It's not *that* much money. And I told her that you didn't know about it."

"Which I didn't."

"Right. So I didn't have to lie to my grandmother."

"Okay. What's the third?"

"Well, two more."

God help me. "Sure..."

"Mama's lonely."

That had me sitting up. "Maria? She said that?"

He nodded. "She thought she'd be okay in her studio apartment, but she misses me."

"And you miss her."

"Right. Now, do you want your mother-in-law living with you?"

"There's a legal suite. She'd have her own space."

He laughed. "Oh God, you have this all worked out."

I waved him off. "What's the third thing? Or is it the fourth?"

"Patience."

"Not a virtue I'm known for."

"That is true." He squeezed my hand. "When Roger and Becca bought their house—just before the birth of their fourth child—everyone pitched in to do the renovations. If I ask, I believe we'd have a pod of Orcas descend to help. We could have your down-to-the-studs home habitable in a short period. With Maria and Becca decorating, I believe it would be livable—and beautiful—in no time." He snapped his fingers.

"Just like that?"

"Just like that."

"It sounds too easy."

He shrugged. "Life can be easy sometimes. If we live in the east end, we'll both have to commute to our jobs and to the stadium."

"We'd manage." I'd spent a few hours thinking about how we might make this work.

"Then let's call the realtor tomorrow. Roger and Becca can arrange a home inspection so everything's ready to go when we get home."

"Just like that?"

"Yeah, just like that." He pressed a kiss to my lips. "Well, first we go to an All-Blacks game."

"You don't want to stay? Play for the best team in the world?"

He tilted his head. "Was that always a dream? Sure. Every kid who plays rugby dreams big. But Canada's my home. And the odds of me making the squad are infinitesimal. The odds of making a happy life with you are so, so, so much better. I like playing to win."

I couldn't believe how simple he made everything sound.

"Are you going to tell Nana, or am I?"

"We'll tell her together."

And the next day, we did.

Epilogue

Isaiah

"**O**kay, like this is…wow."

Becca, the latest infant tucked against her arm, grinned. "Yeah, I thought you'd be impressed."

"We were gone for two weeks. Played three games." I spun around the living room. "I come home and everything's done."

Mama wrapped an arm around my waist. "Your man was particularly helpful."

I arched an eyebrow.

Becca laughed. "We told him what to do, and he did it. You picked the perfect partner."

In more ways than one. Travis might be a pussycat when with others—happy to go along and be amiable. In bed? A dominating tiger who took me to new heights of pleasure every night. Then my words from our last night in New Zealand flashed in my mind. "You be my man now—you're family. You just inherited all these relatives."

He'd understood. Then he'd gotten down on one knee—before Nana and my entire family—and asked me to marry him. Oh, and he'd told me we had Mama's blessing. He'd called and asked her. He'd begged her to fly out for that moment, but she truly couldn't get away.

I'd accepted, of course.

And our first night back in Vancouver, we'd taken Mama out to the Top of Vancouver Restaurant.

In her entire life, she'd never gone to the revolving restaurant.

I loved we were able to give that to her.

I loved that she demanded Travis sit across from her so she could hold his hand on the table and offer a watery smile as she made him promise to take care of me.

Then she'd turned to me and demanded I make the same commitment.

Of course I had. Without hesitation.

We closed on the house the next day.

And wow, it probably should've been torn down. But I loved the old bones and, after seven weeks of intense work, she'd finally been ready for us to move in.

Then I'd gone for the away games.

Travis had stayed behind—promising I'd be thrilled when I returned.

Becca and Mama ensured that happened.

As Mama gave me a tour, she pointed out something each team member had given as a gift. From a vase Jason claimed he'd chosen himself—which I totally believed—to the huge team photo, signed by everyone, that Johnnie had framed.

I'd teared up.

Roger and Becca's gift was a stunning comforter in purples, golds, greens, and blues.

Well, their second gift.

The first had been asking Travis and me to be godparents to their fifth child.

Badarse might've sputtered—pointing out that two atheists as godparents maybe wasn't the best idea.

Becca had pressed her hand to his. "My entire family can teach the baby religion. You can teach her how to live a good life. No matter what befalls her."

I might've blinked back tears.

We might've agreed.

Kristiane Angelique had been born less than a week later at a very healthy nine pounds.

Travis had questioned—to me alone—how *that* worked.

I pointed out I'd been eleven pounds.

He'd winced.

We hadn't discussed the matter since.

My nose twitched.

Travis appeared from the kitchen and grinned. "I didn't hear you come in." He glanced behind him. "Okay, kind of not surprising." He made his way over to me, wrapped his arms around me, and smacked me on the lips.

"Hey!" Mama, of course. She appeared at the doorway to the kitchen. "Where's my kiss?"

Becca nudged me. "Go check out the feast we've made."

"The guys will be here shortly. I was…"

"In a hurry?"

"I might've offered the cabbie more money if he got me here sooner."

Johnnie was grabbing my bag and the rest of the squad were joining us. Thank God this was a big place—but we were still facing standing room only.

"I love you." Travis pulled back to gaze into my eyes. "I didn't know I was allowed to be this happy."

"With me? Always."

I flashed to our simple wedding at the pub where we'd met. Jemi, the bartender, had obtained a license to officiate.

Mama insisted on a priest to bless our union.

Fortunately, the guy'd been pretty hip, choosing to wear a Hawaiian shirt.

As had everyone else, including Travis's friends, Dodge and Annabelle.

Dodge who'd let it slip that Travis was starting as a junior supervisor the next week.

I'd grinned. Because maybe I'd been the one to let Dodge know Travis had taken some courses. And maybe Dodge had been the one to approach the foreman. And since the crew had just lost a supervisor, the foreman had been happy to promote Travis.

A couple of the guys had grumbled.

Everything now, though, had settled.

I didn't really worry less—given he was still at the top of a sky-scraper, but I did like he wasn't putting as much strain on his body.

Which left more energy to regularly put me through my paces. "I love you too. Now, shouldn't we grab food *before* the hungry masses show? Those pretzels on the plane won't have been enough—"

"Honey, we're home." Johnnie's booming voice rang out.

Travis and I met each other's gazes.

"Race you?" He grinned.

"For the rest of our lives."

We hotfooted to the kitchen before my teammates got there first.

Thank you for reading *Hot Rucking Canadian*. The next book in
RUCKED BY YOU is *Sweet Rucking Temptation*.
Check out the rest of our amazing Rugby Romances in this series!
Arrogant Rucking Player
Sweet Rucking Temptation
Star Rucked Lovers
Playing Rucking Hard
Friends Rucked Up
Revamped Rucking Reaper
Big Rucking Deal
(FYI – this is Johnnie's story!)

Want more Gabbi Grey?
Check out her Love in Mission City series, set in beautiful British
Columbia.
The first book is
Ginger Snapping All the Way (Love in Mission City Book 1)

Also available:
Stanley's Christmas Redemption (Love in Mission City Book 2)

The Beauty of the Beast (Love in Mission City Book 2.5)
Sleigh Bells and Second Chances (Love in Mission City Book 3)
A Daddy for Christmas 2: Foster (Love in Mission City Book 3.5)
Rayne's Return (Love in Mission City Book 4)
Gideon's Gratitude (Love in Mission City Book 5)
Love in Mission City: The Boyfriend Gamble
Love in Mission City: The Boyfriends Duet
Love in Mission City: The Shorts
Rayne Check
Archer's Awakening
A Daddy for Christmas 3: Lorcan
Thought You Were the One
Love Without Reservations
Page Against the Machine
The Lightkeeper's Love Affair
Ace's Place
Marcus's Cadence
Not in it for the Money

Also:
Axe to Grind
Grindstone's Edge
Voice to Raise
Hugh (Single Dads of Gaynor Beach)
Anthony (Single Dads of Gaynor Beach)
Xavier (Single Dads of Gaynor Beach)
Love Furever (Friends of Gaynor Beach Animal Rescue)
Husky Love (Friends of Gaynor Beach Animal Rescue)
Yorkie to My Heart (Friends of Gaynor Beach Animal Rescue)
My Past, Your Future

If Only for Today
Catch a Tiger by the Tail
Solstice Surprise
Valentino in Vancouver
You See Me
Sun, Surf, and Surprises
Ginger in the City
Caressa's Homecoming (Bound by Love Book 1)
Cole's Reckoning (Bound by Love Book 2)
An Uncommon Gentleman
A Sensible Gentleman
Didn't See You Coming
Finding Noah (Foggy Basin Season 2)
Unlocked and Unlost

Audiobooks
Ginger Snapping All the Way
Stanley's Christmas Redemption
Sleigh Bells and Second Chances
Rayne Check
Rayne's Return
Thought You Were the One
Love in Mission City: The Shorts
Page Against the Machine
The Lightkeeper's Love Affair
Ace's Place
Marcus's Cadence
Not in it for the Money
Hugh (Single Dads of Gaynor Beach)
Anthony (Single Dads of Gaynor Beach)

Love Furever (Friends of Gaynor Beach Animal Rescue)
Husky Love (Friends of Gaynor Beach Animal Rescue)
My Past, Your Future
If Only for Today
Catch a Tiger by the Tail
Solstice Surprise
An Uncommon Gentleman
A Sensible Gentleman
Didn't See You Coming

Want a free short story? The story is set in Gaynor Beach, California where there are plenty of single dads and puppy rescues! You can sign up for my newsletter so you can keep up with all the great stuff I'm doing as well as pictures of my own pooches, Ally and Finnegan.
Hemingway's Happy Day

Love contemporary MF romances? What's better than love in the beautiful Cedar Valley in British Columbia, Canada? Find small town romances with a touch of angst, a bit of heat, and a lot of heart...
The Absolution of Abigail Reardon (prequel)
The Luminosity of Loriana Harper (Book 1)
The Making of Marnie Jones (Book 2)
The Redemption of Remy St. Claire (Book 3)

Interested in knowing more about Gabbi?

Sign up for her newsletter

Follow her on Bookbub

Follow her on Instagram

USA Today Bestselling author Gabbi Grey lives in beautiful British Columbia where her fur baby chin-poo keeps her safe from the nasty neighborhood squirrels. Working for the government by day, she spends her early mornings writing contemporary, gay, sweet, and dark erotic BDSM romances. While she firmly believes in happy endings, she also believes in making her characters suffer before finding their true love. She also writes m/f romances as Gabbi Black and Gabbi Powell.